"I hear we're having an affair."

Fiona turned as red as her hair. "We're not!"

"I know."

"It's ridiculous!" She was pacing now, waving her hands, color still brilliant in her cheeks. "It's because they saw you leaving here in the morning. They think you spent the night!"

"I did."

"They think you slept with me!"

"Not a bad idea," he murmured.

"The whole damn island thinks that I'm your mistress!"

Lachlan grinned at her. "Now, there's an even better idea!"

Harlequin Presents® is proud to bring you
a brand-new trilogy from international
bestselling author

ANNE McALLISTER

Welcome to

The McGillivrays of Pelican Cay

Meet:
Lachlan McGillivray—he's ready to take his
pretend mistress to bed!
Hugh McGillivray—is about to claim a bride....
Molly McGillivray—her Spanish lover is ready
to surrender to passion!

Visit:
the stunning tropical island of Pelican Cay—
full of sun-drenched beaches,
it's the perfect place for passion!

Don't miss this fantastic new trilogy:
McGillivray's Mistress—November 2003 (#2357)

And coming soon in Harlequin Presents®:
Hugh's story
Molly's story

Anne McAllister

McGILLIVRAY'S MISTRESS

Pelican Cay

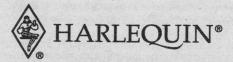

HARLEQUIN®

TORONTO • NEW YORK • LONDON
AMSTERDAM • PARIS • SYDNEY • HAMBURG
STOCKHOLM • ATHENS • TOKYO • MILAN • MADRID
PRAGUE • WARSAW • BUDAPEST • AUCKLAND

For Cathy and Steve the best of friends
For Sid, the finest of felines
For Bob, Dyl and Spiff, who have to put up with him
And for Ange and Sparks whose head
definitely won't fit through the cat flap after this!

With thanks to Gail Chavenelle, whose sculptures inspired
Fiona's and who so generously shared her expertise with me

ISBN 0-373-12357-4

McGILLIVRAY'S MISTRESS

First North American Publication 2003.

Copyright © 2003 by Barbara Schenck.

CHAPTER ONE

SOME PEOPLE called it "sculpture." Lachlan McGillivray begged to differ.

As far as he was concerned, the monstrosity on the beach in front of his elegant upscale Moonstone Inn was—pure and simple—"trash."

What else could you possibly call the nightmare—ten feet high and growing—that had begun to arise a month ago from the flotsam and jetsam that washed up on Pelican Cay's beautiful pink sand beach?

"Delightfully inventive," an article in last Sunday's Nassau paper called it. "A creative amalgam," the Freeport newspaper had said. "Fresh and thought-provoking," the art critic from a far-reaching Florida daily claimed.

"Deliberate nose-thumbing," was Lachlan's opinion. It was just Fiona Dunbar having a go at him.

Again.

Fiona Dunbar had been a pain in the posterior—*his* posterior!—since he and his family had moved to the small Bahamian island when Lachlan was fifteen.

Life in suburban Virginia with its soccer leagues and its supply of cute blonde cheerleaders had been all he'd ever wanted back then. Being uprooted and transplanted to a remote Caribbean island just so his father could satisfy a need for wanderlust at the same time that he pursued his career as a family physician had infuriated Lachlan, though the rest of the family had come willingly enough.

In fact his brother, Hugh, two years younger, and his

sister, Molly, six years his junior, had been delighted to
trade their stateside existence for life in the sticks.

"There's nothing to do there!" Lachlan had complained.

"Exactly," his father had said happily, looking around
at the miles of deserted beach and the softly breaking waves
and then up the hill at the higgledy-piggledy scatter of pastel-colored houses, its 350-year-old rusting cannon, and the
half-overgrown cricket field with its resident grass-mowing
horse. "That's just the point."

Lachlan hadn't been able to see it then. He'd thought it
was the most boring place on earth, and he'd said so often.

"So leave," Molly's best friend, the supremely irritating
Fiona Dunbar had said, sticking her tongue out at him.

"Believe me, carrots, I would if I could," he'd replied.

And he had—as soon as his acceptance had come from
the University of Virginia. He'd been gone four years, returning only occasionally to see his parents. Then he'd gone
on to Europe to play soccer in England, Spain and Italy,
and had come back even less often, and then only to regale
family and friends with tales of life in the fast lane.

But oddly, the longer he was gone, the more he found
himself remembering the good things about Pelican Cay.
The more he'd awakened in the morning in this big city or
that one and listened to the birds cough, the more fondly
he'd remembered waking to island birds and island breezes.
The more he moved frenetically from one place to another,
the more he appreciated the slower island pace. He liked
the autobahn and the Louvre and the centuries of European
culture. He liked French cuisine and Italian delicacies and
Spanish wines. But sometimes he missed a slow amble
down a potholed road, a one-room island historical society,
the 350-year-old rusty cannon, a plate of conch fritters and
a long cold beer.

A couple of years ago, when Hugh had come back to
start his island charter service, Fly Guy, in Pelican Cay,
even though their parents had moved back to Virginia,
Lachlan had thought his brother had the right idea.

"I'll probably come back when I retire, too," he'd said. Hugh had raised dark brows. "And do what?"

Hugh had gone to college, then into the U.S. Navy where he'd been a pilot for eight years. But always a beachcomber at heart, he'd finally bolted the regimented world and was never happier than when he was lying in a hammock, drinking a beer and watching the waves wash up on the shore.

That was not Lachlan. Lachlan had always had goals. He'd made up his mind at the age of twelve that he was going to be "the best damn goalkeeper" in the world and he'd never swerved from his pursuit of that.

While his parents had scowled at his profanity, they'd admired his determination—and his success. He'd spent sixteen years as one of the best goalkeepers in the world. But even he couldn't play in goal forever.

It was a young man's game. A young *healthy* man's game. Retirement had come last summer, at the age of thirty-four, when a serious knee injury had so compromised his quickness that Lachlan knew it was time. His mind was as quick as ever, his anticipation as great. But he would never get his edge back physically. And he refused to play down a level.

There was only one place to be—at the top.

Fortunately, he'd been buying up real estate for the past four years. Eighteen months ago he'd decided on his post-soccer career and had, with his customary determination, set about accomplishing it. First he'd bought the Mirabelle, a small elegant inn at the far end of Pelican Cay. It was already a thriving business and he could step right in when-ever he wanted to. That made sense to everyone.

But when the Moonstone, then called the Sand Dollar, came on the market and he bought that, everyone had been appalled.

"What the hell are you going to do with that?" Hugh had demanded. The eighty-year-old, three-story clapboard structure with its peeling paint and sagging verandas had looked like nothing but work to him.

"I'll restore it and refurbish it," Lachlan had said, relishing the prospect.

"What do you know about building restoration?" Hugh raised skeptical brows.

And Lachlan had had to admit he'd known very little. But the challenge drove him. He'd thrown himself into it with vigor and enthusiasm. He'd learned and studied and worked. He'd hired lots of help, but he'd been right in there doing his part, determined to "turn it into the best damn inn in the Caribbean." It had been open over a year now, and was doing very well.

"Pretty soon," Lachlan had told Hugh not long ago, "it will become the destination of choice for active discriminating travelers, those who have the brains and the soul to appreciate the true beauty of the islands."

Hugh had stopped humming along with Jimmy Buffett long enough to look up from his hammock and laugh. "The way you appreciated it?"

But Lachlan just shrugged him off. "You'll see. It will be great. For the tourists and for the island. The Mirabelle will still take the old guard—those folks who have been coming for years. But the Moonstone will attract the newcomers. And that will be good for Pelican Cay. The island could use a kick in the butt. Something has to jumpstart the economy. Fishing's not enough now. They need to diversify and—"

"The zeal of the converted," Hugh had shaken his head and closed his eyes.

Which was true enough, Lachlan supposed. As much as he'd resented Pelican Cay all those years ago, all he could see were possibilities now—

And a ten-foot monstrosity every time he opened the blinds.

He scowled out the window again. The monster seemed to have gained another arm overnight. A bent driftwood spar thrust upward from its side, and something not quite discernible in the early morning half-light fluttered from its outflung hand.

Plastic? Seaweed? Whatever it was, it taunted him.

He turned away again and flung himself into the chair at his desk and tried to focus on the correspondence that his assistant and the Moonstone's manager, Suzette, had left for him to sign and the mail that had arrived while he was gone.

He'd been away since Saturday, having flown to the Abacos to oversee some renovations at the Sandpiper, the next in the series of inns he was renovating. He'd returned very late last night and had deliberately avoided glancing at the *thing* when Maurice, one of the island's taxi drivers, had dropped him off at the door.

Bad enough that he'd felt compelled to open the blinds this morning to see what further effrontery Fiona had achieved.

He tried to ignore it and get back to the business at hand. He had plenty of pressing things to worry about. But his fingers strangled his pen as he scanned and signed half a dozen letters, then read the post that had arrived since he'd left.

The last one was a response to a letter he'd dictated in the spring. The Moonstone had done well all on its own during the winter months. Sun-seeking snowbirds from the northern climes had filled the rooms every night. But summer and fall occupancy was more problematic. So he'd sent notice of its existence to several exclusive tour agencies and travel magazines, encouraging them to send a representative to see what the Moonstone had to offer.

A couple of the tour companies had, including the impressive Grantham Cultural Tours whose founder was arriving later this week. This particular letter, however, was a response from an upscale travel magazine called *Island Vistas*.

"Will be arriving next week," the tour rep had written. "The 'quiet island elegance' you mention hits exactly the right note. The Moonstone sounds exactly like the sort of place our readers love.''

Quiet island elegance! Oh yeah, right. With a ten-foot steeple of trash growing on its doorstep?

''Well, it's quiet,'' Hugh had said cheerfully last week when Lachlan had complained about it. He was enjoying Fiona's tactics as they weren't aimed at him. ''Doesn't make a sound. Does it?''

It didn't have to. It was a visual scream. It was an affront to him—and to the sensibilities of the inn's guests. And if that wasn't annoyance enough, there were always the bagpipes.

''Bagpipes?'' Hugh had stared at him.

''Wait,'' Lachlan had raised a hand to still his brother's protest. ''Just wait.''

And after they'd eaten in the inn's dining room, he'd insisted Hugh sit on the deck of the Moonstone and wait until night fell on Pelican Cay—and the miserable tremulous bleat and warble of an off-key *Garryowen* drifted toward them on the breeze.

Hugh's stunned expression had given Lachlan considerable satisfaction. But he would gladly have forgone it, for the pleasure of hearing nothing but the waves breaking on the sand. He arched his brows to say *Now do you believe me?*

''You don't know it's Fiona.''

''Who the hell else could it possibly be?''

Fiona Dunbar had been systematically driving him crazy since she was nine years old.

She and his sister, Molly, were the same age and, from the moment they met, had become best friends. Why he— a mature and lordly fifteen at the time—should have had to suffer being constantly plagued by two grubby-faced, sassy, stubborn little monsters was beyond him.

But he had been. Molly and Fiona had followed him everywhere, dogging his footsteps, pestering him continually, watching everything he did—*spying on him!*—and wanting to do it, too.

"Be nice to them," his mother had admonished time and time again. "They're just little girls."

Little demons, more like. And regardless of his mother's strictures, Lachlan had done his best to chase them away. He'd snarled at them, growled at them, roared at them. He'd threatened them and slammed his bedroom door on them. But they'd persisted.

"They admire you," his mother had said.

"They're trying to drive me crazy," Lachlan replied.

But nothing had got rid of them until the day Fiona had heard him telling a college girl he'd met on the beach how awful it was living on Pelican Cay and how glad he'd be to leave.

"It's the end of the earth," he'd said. "There's nothing worth having here."

"So leave," Fiona had blurted, her fury turning her complexion as red as her hair.

As he hadn't been talking to her—hadn't even realized she was nearby—he and the girl he'd been talking to had both stared at her in surprise.

"Just get on a boat and get out of here," Fiona had gone on angrily. "Or better yet, swim. Maybe you'll drown! Go to hell, Lachlan McGillivray!" And she'd spun away and run down the beach.

"Who's that?" the blonde had asked him. "And what's her problem?"

Lachlan, embarrassed, had shrugged. "Who knows? That's Fiona. She's just a nutty kid."

And he would be extremely glad when she grew up!

Or at least he'd thought he would be.

Somehow, though, Fiona Dunbar, all grown-up, turned out to be worse.

Her stick-straight body had developed curves somewhere along the way. Her carroty red hair, which back then had been ruthlessly tamed into a long ponytail, had, in the past couple of years, become a free loose fiery curtain of auburn silk that begged to be touched. As did her skin which was creamy except where it was golden with freckles. And that was the most perverse thing of all—even her freckles enticed him!

It wasn't fair.

He hadn't come back to Pelican Cay to notice Fiona Dunbar! Perversely, though, he couldn't seem to help it. She was here. She was unattached. And she was, by far, the most beautiful woman on the island.

But unlike every other woman between the ages of seven and seventy—virtually all of whom had fallen all over themselves trying to impress Lachlan McGillivray during his soccer-playing career—Fiona Dunbar wanted nothing to do with him.

So he wasn't God's gift to *all* women. Lachlan still had had more than his share of groupies over the years. And while he didn't think he was drop-dead handsome, women seemed to like his deep blue eyes, his crooked grin and his hard dark looks.

Wherever he'd gone, certainly plenty of women had followed—chatting him up in bars, tucking their phone numbers in the pockets of his shirts and trousers, ringing him at all hours of the day and night, clamoring to be the one in his bed on any given night—even offering him their underwear!

Four years ago, at the height of Lachlan's popularity, a magazine interviewer witnessing a woman doing just that, had asked him if that sort of thing happened often.

"Well, sometimes," Lachlan had admitted honestly because it was only the truth. And then because that sounded arrogant, he'd joked, "But I only keep the red ones."

And just like that, dear God, an urban legend had been born!

Two days after the magazine hit the stands the first pair of red panties arrived in his mail. Dozens more followed. He'd been deluged—at his home, at the club, at the hotels on the road. More stories followed. And so did more pairs of panties. Before long every scandal sheet across Europe was filled with women claiming their panties were the centerpiece of Lachlan McGillivray's collection.

It didn't matter that none of it was true, it was a great story.

Next thing he knew he had a worldwide fan club whose membership was three-quarters women. The club sent out thousands of autographed pictures of him leaping, legs and arms outstretched, to make a spectacular save.

"They admire my ability," Lachlan said modestly whenever he had been asked about the extent of his popularity.

"They admire your legs," his sister Molly had said flatly, shaking her head at the extent of female idiocy. "Men in shorts! Some women just can't get enough of them."

Most women, in Lachlan's experience.

Not Fiona Dunbar.

She hated him. Eighteen months ago she'd proved it. He and a couple of his teammates had come to Pelican Cay to visit his brother, Hugh, over Christmas. Molly had gone to see their parents in Virginia, but because he had work to do in the islands, Hugh couldn't go. So, feeling a bit homesick, he had invited his brother to visit him for the holidays.

"Not that I expect you to come," he'd said cavalierly. "I'm sure you've got plenty of other more fascinating places to go."

Lachlan had. Between the demands of goalkeeping and his frenetic social life—even without the red panties collection it was pretty hectic—there was rarely a dull moment. That Christmas he'd gone to Monaco to live it up day and night with a girl called Lisette. Or was it Claudine? Suzanne?

Or all of the above. The fact was, there had been plenty—more than plenty—of willing women.

Two days before New Year's, though, exhausted from a season of hard work and a holiday of hard play, he thought that spending a week or so of solitary celibate days on a deserted pink sand beach sounded like heaven.

He'd said as much to Joaquin Santiago and Lars Erik Lindquist, two of his equally hard-driving, hard-living teammates. And twenty-four hours later, the three of them had arrived on Pelican Cay.

Still hung over when Hugh met them in Nassau, Lachlan had sworn, "No booze. No babes. Just sand and sun and sleep." And at his brother's disbelieving look, he'd yawned and nodded as firmly as his aching head would permit. "My New Year's resolutions."

Bad news, then, that the first person he saw later that day was a Titian-haired beauty in a bikini sashaying past Hugh's tiny house, heading toward the beach.

"Who the hell is that?"

"Fiona," Hugh said offhandedly. "Dunbar," he'd added at Lachlan's blank look. "You remember—Molly's friend."

"Fiona?" Lachlan's voice had cracked with disbelief. "*That's* Fiona Dunbar?" That total knockout?

Hugh grinned. "Doesn't much look like Fiona the ferret these days, does she?" That was what they had dubbed her at age ten, when she and Molly the mole had been sneaking around after them every day.

Lachlan sucked air. No, she didn't look much like Fiona the ferret. She looked drop-dead gorgeous. Delectable. Beddable.

His "no babes" resolution began to crack. He kept an eye out for her after that. But while he saw her frequently over the next few days, she never came near.

She was taking care of her father, Hugh told him. A former fisherman, Tom Dunbar had had a stroke some years back, not long after Fiona had graduated from high school. She'd spent the next ten years taking care of him.

"And working," Hugh said. "She works at Carin Campbell's gift shop. And she sculpts."

"Sculpts?" Lachlan had looked doubtful.

"Oh yeah. Sand sculptures. Shells. Even metal. Cuts them and bends them into shape—like paper dolls."

Lachlan couldn't imagine. But he wandered down to Carin's shop later that day to buy some postcards, and he found quite a few of Fiona's pieces. He had to admit they were pretty impressive—pelicans and other shore birds, palm trees and hammocks and fishermen. She was selling sketches there, too. And caricatures.

Then he realized that the witty sculpture Hugh had hanging in his house—one of him looping the loop in his seaplane—was a Fiona Dunbar piece, as was the caricature of Maurice at the custom's house taxi stand, and the one of Miss Saffron the straw lady which he spotted hanging on her porch.

She drew caricatures of tourists and sold them the sketches on the beach. She even drew Lars Erik and Joaquin as they'd ogled the bikini-clad women on the beach. He knew that because Lars Erik had bought it from her.

She drew everybody and their dog. But she never drew him.

It rankled. Lachlan didn't like being ignored—particularly when he hadn't managed to ignore her.

Finally, when a week had gone by and she hadn't even said hello to him, he'd had enough, especially since he'd just told Joaquin and Lars Erik that he'd known her for years.

"I don't believe it," Lars Erik said.

They were sitting in the Grouper, drinking beer, and Fiona had just come in, carrying a folder with some sketches in it, which she'd hugged against her breasts as she scanned the room. She'd spared Lars Erik a brief smile, but had skipped right over Lachlan as if he were invisible.

"She's just miffed because a long time ago I didn't like her precious island," he explained.

"Oh, right," Lars Erik said, nodding his head.

"Probably doesn't even know her," Joaquin speculated with a sly grin.

"Of course I know her. She's a friend of my sister's. Her name is Fiona Dunbar. Isn't it?" he said to the bartender.

The bartender, Maurice's son Michael, grinned broadly. "That be Fiona, all right."

"So you know her name," Lars Erik said. "So what? Invite her over to have a drink with us."

"He doesn't know her," Joaquin said.

So he had to prove it. With Joaquin and Lars Erik egging him on, he'd strode over to where Fiona had just handed a pair of sketches to a tourist couple. He smiled his best charm-the-ladies smile and invited her to have a drink with him.

She blinked, then shook her head. "With you? I don't think so."

He stared at her, astonished at her refusal. "What do you mean, you don't think so?" He was annoyed that she'd said no, more annoyed that she didn't seem to recognize him, and most annoyed by the fact that the closer he got to her the more gorgeous she became.

He wanted to see flaws. There weren't any.

"Maybe you don't remember me." It was possible, he supposed. He didn't think he'd changed that much, but she sure as hell didn't look the way she used to!

"Oh, I remember you," she said, and gave him a blinding smile as she slipped between him and the barstool. "That's why I don't want to."

And leaving him standing there staring after her, Fiona sashayed out the door, letting it swing shut after her.

Behind him, over the sounds of the steel drum band playing "Yellow Bird," Lachlan heard Joaquin and Lars Erik hooting.

"Well, helloooo, darlin'," a sultry voice sounded in his ear, and Lachlan turned to see a busty blonde sitting on the barstool behind him.

"Hello, yourself," he said, teeth still clenched, but managing a smile to meet her own.

She put a hand on his arm and slid off the stool to stand next to him, almost pressed against him. "You're Lachlan, aren't you? The one they call 'the gorgeous goalie'?"

"Some people have said that." He rubbed the back of his neck.

"Some people are very perceptive," the blonde purred. She smiled. "I was just heading out for a little walk on the beach. Want to go for a swim?"

"Why not?" It sounded a hell of a lot more appealing than listening to Joaquin and Lars Erik snickering into their beers. He looped an arm around the blonde's shoulders and steered her out the door.

Fiona, after her grand exit, hadn't gone far. He spotted her standing on the porch of the gift shop talking to Carin. She didn't look his way.

Lachlan looked hers—and gave her a long slow smug smile as he and the blonde walked past.

"I knew I'd get lucky," the blonde was giggling. "I've got my red panties on tonight."

Deliberately Lachlan nibbled the blonde's ear. "Not for long," he promised her.

He didn't remember whether she'd been wearing red panties or not. He didn't remember anything about her. He'd gone back to England two days later—and the only thing he remembered from the holiday was blasted annoying Fiona!

"The fish that got away," Joaquin called her.

"Like letting in a goal," Lars Erik said, "when you've kept a clean sheet."

"We'll see about that," Lachlan muttered.

He hadn't had time then. But when he came back this past winter, sailing over on the boat he'd bought in Nassau, making plans to move to the island permanently that spring, he'd taken another shot.

Hugh had been going out with a model he'd met who

was doing a honeymoon photo shoot, so Lachlan had suggested a double date—a *blind* double date.

"Why not?" He'd made the suggestion casually. "Just ask Fiona Whatshername along."

Hugh had raised his eyebrows. "She's busy with her dad."

"I'll get someone to stay with her dad," Lachlan had said. "It will be good for her." He arranged for Maurice to go by and play dominos with Tom Dunbar and Hugh did the asking.

To say that Fiona had been surprised when Lachlan had been the one to pick her up would have been putting it mildly. She looked stricken when he turned up on the doorstep. Then she said, relieved, "Oh, you must have come to see my dad—"

"No. I'm here for you."

"But—"

She looked like she might protest. But in the end, she'd let herself be drawn out on to the porch and down the steps. "We're meeting Hugh and his girl at Beaches."

"Beaches?" Fiona's eyes widened.

Beaches was the nicest place on the island. Not a place Hugh could afford.

"I'll pay," Lachlan had told him. "You want to impress this girl, don't you?"

"Yeah. But…" Hugh had shaken his head. "Do you want to impress Fiona Dunbar?"

Lachlan hadn't known what he wanted to do with Fiona Dunbar. Then. Later that night he'd known exactly what he wanted—

He hadn't got it.

She'd damned near drowned him instead.

These days he wasn't touching Fiona Dunbar with a ten-foot pole!

Other than the sympathy note he'd sent when Hugh had told him of her father's death in March, he'd had no communication with her at all. In fact, ever since he'd moved into the Moonstone a month ago, he'd done his best to avoid her.

Of course he still noticed her. Hard not to when the island wasn't that big and she was *still* the most gorgeous woman around. But he didn't have to have anything to do with her. Pelican Cay was big enough for both of them.

Try telling Fiona Dunbar that.

Less than a week after he'd opened the Moonstone, a letter to the editor had appeared in the local paper decrying the "standard branding" of the island. Fiona Dunbar, signing herself "a concerned citizen" made it sound like he was singlehandedly trying to undermine local culture.

For God's sake, he was trying to salvage an abandoned architectural treasure and turn it into something tasteful and profitable before time and the weather reduced it to kindling—out of which the artistic Ms. Dunbar would doubtless construct one of her bloody sculptures!

Tactfully as possible, he had attempted a letter to the editor of his own in reply.

A week later there had been another letter, this time about the local youth soccer team.

"People who are going to take advantage of local amenities," the perennially concerned Ms. Dunbar had written, "should be willing to contribute their skills—however meager—to the betterment of the island's children."

Him, she meant. Teach them soccer, she meant.

"Well, it is how you made your millions," Hugh pointed out.

"It would be such a great thing for the kids," Carin Campbell agreed.

So did Maurice and Estelle. Their grandsons would love a soccer team with a real coach for a change.

"Or don't you think you can?" Molly had said in that baiting little-sisterly way she could still dredge up in a pinch.

Of course he damned well could.

And so he had. For the past month Lachlan had spent

hours with a rag-tag bunch of ten- to fifteen-year-old kids who called themselves the Pelicans. The Pelicans were never going to win the World Cup, but they were a lot more capable now than they had been when he'd started working with them. Marcus Cash was turning into a pretty decent striker, Tom Dunbar, Fiona's nephew, was a good defender, and Maurice's grandson, Lorenzo, had the makings of a born goalkeeper.

Lachlan was proud of them. He was proud of himself as their coach. He was a damned good teacher, and he'd have liked Fiona the ferret to see that—but she'd never once come to watch them play.

She never said a word to him.

She didn't have to. Her sculpture said it all.

Lachlan shoved himself up from his chair and stalked across the room to glare once again at her message.

And as the full morning sun illuminated Fiona Dunbar's trash masterpiece, he saw what he'd been unable to make out before—the pair of red women's panties that flapped—like a red flag in front of a bull—from the sculpture's outstretched arm.

THE POUNDING ON HER DOOR woke her.

Fiona groaned, then pried open an eyelid and peered at the clock: 7:22.

7:22? Who in God's name could possibly want to talk to her at 7:22 in the morning? No one who knew her, that was for sure.

Never an early riser, Fiona preferred to start her day when the sun was high in the sky.

It was why she was a sculptor not a painter, she'd told her friend Carin Campbell more than once.

Painters needed to worry about light. Sculptors could work any old time.

Obviously whoever was banging on the door wasn't aware that she'd been working all night long.

She'd labored until well past midnight on the pieces she

sold in Carin's shop—the metal cutouts and seashell miniatures that were her bread and butter. The paper doll silhouettes she cut and bent and the tiny exquisite sculptures made out of coquina shells, sea glass, bits of driftwood and pebbles were tourist favorites. Easy to transport and immediately evocative of Pelican Cay, they paid the bills and allowed her to keep the old story-and-a-half pink house on the quay that overlooked the harbor.

Normally she finished about two. But last night after she'd done two pelicans, a fisherman, a surfer and a week's worth of miniature pelicans and dolphins and flying fish and the odd coconut palm or two, she had just begun.

Of course she could have gone to bed, but instead she'd gathered up the treasures she'd found on the shoreline after high tide—the driftwood spar, the sun lotion bottle, the kelp and flipflop and…other things…and set off to add them to her sculpture on the beach.

She hadn't got home until four.

"All right, already," she muttered as the pounding continued. She stretched and flexed aching shoulders, then hauled herself up, pulled on a pair of shorts to go with the T-shirt she slept in and padded downstairs to the door. "Hold your horses."

If it was some befuddled tourist, hung over from a late night at the Grouper and still looking for the house he'd rented for the week, she was going to be hard-pressed to be civil.

Yanking open the door, she began frostily, "Are you aware—?"

And stopped as her words dried up and she found herself staring up into the furious face of Lachlan McGillivray.

He didn't speak, just thrust something at her. Something small and wadded up and bright red.

Fiona bit back the sudden smile that threatened to touch her lips.

"Yours, I presume?" he drawled.

Fiona snatched them and started to shut the door, but Lachlan pushed past her into the room.

"What do you think you're doing? I didn't invite you in."

"Didn't you? Seems to me you've been inviting me a lot." He was smiling but it was one of those smiles that sharks had before they ate people.

"I never—!"

A dark brow lifted. "No? Then why put that monstrosity in front of the Moonstone?"

"It's not a monstrosity!"

"That's a matter of opinion. Why there?"

"It's a public beach."

"There are three miles of public beach."

"I can put it anywhere I want."

"Exactly. And you wanted to put it in front of the Moonstone."

"So?" Fiona lifted her chin. "You should be glad," she told him. "I'm raising the artistic consciousness of your guests."

He snorted. "Right. You're saving them from standard brands, aren't you?" He made it sound like she was an idiot.

Fiona wrapped her arms across her chest. "That's one way of putting it," she said loftily.

"Another way is saying you're draining away the life blood of the island economy," Lachlan told her.

"I am not! I would *never* hurt the island!" Trust a jerk like Lachlan McGillivray to completely misunderstand the whole reason behind her efforts. "This is *my* home," she told him. "I was the one who was born here! I'm the one who's never left!"

"And that makes you better than everyone else?"

"Of course not."

"Just better than me."

"You hate it here," she reminded him.

"Hated it," he corrected her. "Hell's bells, Fiona. I was

fifteen years old. I'd been dragged away from my home to some godforsaken island in the middle of the ocean. I missed my friends. I missed playing soccer. I didn't want to be here!''

She pressed her lips together, resisting his words. Of course they made sense now, as they hadn't back then. Back then she'd taken them personally, as she'd taken everything Lachlan McGillivray had done personally.

''Even so,'' she said stubbornly. ''You didn't have to come back.''

''I wanted to come back.''

But she didn't want him back! She was *over* Lachlan McGillivray! At least she'd thought she was—until that night he'd taken her to Beaches.

''And I'm staying,'' he went on inexorably. ''Whether you like it or not, I'm here and the Moonstone's here, and we're going to stay.''

''I don't care if the Moonstone is here. I'm *glad* it's here!'' At least she would have been if Lachlan weren't the one running it. And as for Lachlan staying, she doubted that.

Lachlan was glitz-and-glamour personified. He'd lived in England, in Italy, in Spain. He'd dined with kings and dated supermodels. He was not the sort of man to settle down on a tiny out-of-the-way Caribbean island.

She just wished he would hurry up and leave!

And he could obviously read her mind. Slowly Lachlan shook his head. ''I'm not going anywhere, babe. But that sculpture is.''

Fiona's jaw tightened. Her chin thrust out. ''No.''

''Look, Fiona, I can take a joke as well as the next guy, but...''

''It's not a joke!''

Lachlan rolled his eyes, then looked pointedly at the pair of red bikini panties in her hand.

Instinctively Fiona's fingers tightened around them.

''I found them,'' she said stubbornly. ''On the beach.

Fortuitous, I admit. But I didn't use anything that I didn't find. That's the challenge of it, don't you see?''

Obviously he didn't. He was looking flinty and stubborn, glowering the way he always glowered at opponents on the soccer pitch.

"It's a challenge," she repeated.

"I don't need any more challenges, thank you very much."

"Not to you. To me!"

"What's that supposed to mean?"

Fiona wetted her lips. She hadn't put it into words before, hadn't dared. It seemed presumptuous even now. She wasn't a sculptor. Not really. She'd never had classes, never studied with anyone. What she did with her shells and sand and steel was craft, not art. But she was fascinated with it. "It's...teaching me things."

"Trash is teaching you things?" he said mockingly. "What? Recycling?"

"Composition. Balance. Development. Flexibility. Imagination." She tried to think of all the abstract artistic terms she could use to explain the things that her nighttime creation had been teaching her.

"Yeah, right."

It didn't take any imagination at all to know that Lachlan didn't believe a word of it.

"It's what I do," she said desperately. "I make those little sculptures to sell to the tourists. I cut out metal. I cast sand. I glue rocks. But that's not all I want to do. I want to be a sculptor," she whispered. "A real one."

It wasn't something she had ever admitted before. Hadn't dared to. And she felt like an imposter when she said it now. It had been her dream, of course, long ago—when she'd still had dreams. Once upon a time she'd even thought she might go away to study.

But that had been years ago. Before her father's stroke. Since then she'd been on the island. She'd worked with what the island gave her, learned what it had to teach her. And didn't ask for more.

"You could go back to it," her brother Mike had told her after their dad had passed away.

"You ought to," her brother Paul had encouraged. "Apply for a course somewhere."

But Fiona had shaken her head. "I'm too old. I have a life right here."

"You need to do something," both her brothers had told her. "Dad would want you to. He wouldn't want to think you'd given up everything for him."

"I didn't!" she protested. "I *wanted* to take care of him."

"And you did," Mike said soothingly. "And God knows we all appreciate it. But now you can move on."

It had been three months since her dad's death and she hadn't moved on at all. She'd been grieving, she told herself. She needed time. And a challenge.

The sculpture on the beach had been that challenge. It had brought her to life again. And if it had annoyed Lachlan, well, that had been an added benefit.

"You want to be a sculptor?" Lachlan said doubtfully now.

"Yes."

His hard blue gaze narrowed on her. "And that's what your monstrosity is? A learning experience?"

She nodded. "I call him *The King of the Beach.*"

Lachlan's mouth twisted. "Well, you've been doing him for weeks now. Isn't the challenge gone?"

"There's always new material."

"So use it somewhere else."

Fiona shook her head. "It's a challenge to use it there, to make it part of the whole."

"Find a new challenge."

"Like what?"

"How the hell should I know? You're the one who wants to sculpt!"

"Yes, but I need subjects. I need material. I need to do things I haven't done before. To broaden my horizons!"

God knew it was the truth. She'd never been anywhere or done anything compared to most people. She'd spent her whole life, except for a handful of trips to Nassau and Miami, right here on Pelican Cay. "If I'm going to grow as an artist, I need to tackle new projects, explore different media."

Lachlan's fingers flexed and relaxed. He bounced a little on the balls of his feet. He looked the way he always had in goal when a striker was heading his way.

"So," he said, "if you had something else you wanted to sculpt, something that would challenge you, you'd do that?"

"I—"

"And you'd get rid of that monstrosity on my beach?"

"It's not—"

"Call it what you want. I want it gone. But if you really mean what you said...if you really want to sculpt and not just play games...if you really want a challenge, I have a deal for you."

Fiona eyed him suspiciously. "What deal?"

"You want to be a sculptor, fine. You want new challenges, great. Go for it. Whatever you want to sculpt, I'll provide it. We can add a little 'culture' to the island. And in return, you take down the monstros—The King of the Beach." He looked at her expectantly.

Fiona hesitated. Possibilities reeled through her mind. Hopes. Dreams. Fears.

Lachlan grinned at her, challenging her, like the goalkeeper he was. "Or maybe it's all bull, Fiona. Maybe you're just a prankster, and not really a sculptor at all."

Her spine stiffened. She met his gaze defiantly. "Anything?" she asked. "I can sculpt anything I want?"

He shrugged, still grinning that satisfied grin. "Anything."

"Then I want to sculpt you. Nude."

CHAPTER TWO

"Or maybe *you're* not up to the challenge?" she suggested, the faint smile on her face now turning into an unholy grin.

Lachlan felt as if he'd been blindsided, as if he'd dived to stop the ball—and it had gone zinging past his feet as he'd lunged the other way.

Nude? Had she said she wanted to sculpt him *nude?*

Yes, she had.

But she didn't mean it. Couldn't mean it. She had to be kidding.

But she didn't look like she was kidding.

She looked like she was daring him. There was a sparkle of mischief in Fiona Dunbar's wide green eyes, a blatant challenge in the look she gave him.

Lachlan felt his teeth come together with a snap.

She hadn't wanted him nude once before, damn it. She'd very nearly drowned them both to prevent any such occurrence!

And now—?

"Right. Very funny," Lachlan said tersely and spun away.

Soft but distinct gobbling chicken sounds followed him.

He jerked back around and glared at her.

Fiona stood in guileless silence and stared back. He looked at her closely. There was determination in her gaze—and defiance. And just a hint of something else.

Vulnerability?

No way. Impossible. Fiona Dunbar was about as vulnerable as an asp.

So what was she playing at?

A charcoal gray cat jumped past him suddenly and walked along the table behind Fiona. It came up to her and nudged her with its head. Without breaking eye contact with him, Fiona reached around and scooped the cat into her arms—like a witch with her familiar.

The cat stared at him with watchful green eyes. So did the woman.

Lachlan felt a muscle in his temple tick.

"So you want me nude?" he said at last with all the casual curiosity he could muster. He was gratified to see the color rise in her cheeks.

"*I* don't want you nude," Fiona denied swiftly. "I want to sculpt—"

"Sure. Of course you do," he said sarcastically.

She hugged the cat tighter, as if it were a shield. "You're the one who offered," she pointed out. "Anything you want to sculpt, you said."

"I meant—"

"Of course I'll understand if you've changed your mind," she added archly as she focused on scratching the cat under the chin. "You might not want to bare all. I understand that men who aren't particularly well, er…" She flicked a glance below his belt.

Enough was enough. "You want to see how well-endowed I am?" he asked softly with more than a hint of menace.

"I want to sculpt—"

"Fine," he snapped. "When do you want to do it? Now?" He reached for his belt. She wasn't the only one who could throw down a challenge. She might have scored first with her little "I want to sculpt you nude" line, but the game wasn't over yet.

"No!" she yelped. "I mean, no," she said in more moderate tones. "Not…now. I can't…now. I…I have to get some…some clay first."

"Some clay?" he mocked her.

"Clay," she repeated with a quick jerky nod. "I've never done terra-cotta. I don't have it on hand."

"Right." He didn't believe it for a minute. Oh, he believed she didn't have any on hand. But he didn't believe she really wanted to sculpt him. She was scoring a point. Making him squirm. Wishing him gone.

But he wasn't going anywhere and it was time she realized that.

"Get plenty," he instructed her.

"What?" She blinked and half a dozen expressions flickered across her face.

"If you're going to sculpt me," he challenged her. He saw consternation on her face. Was that panic? Resolution? Determination? He couldn't sort them all out.

Then she squared her shoulders. "I will," she said after a moment. "Hugh can bring it from Nassau when he goes on Wednesday."

Now it was his turn to gulp. Then he got a grip and managed a credibly nonchalant shrug. "Whatever you say." It wasn't going to happen no matter what she said. "Look, Fiona. What do you really—"

"So how about Thursday morning?"

He hadn't expected her to set a date. "Fiona, we're not—"

Soft chicken gobbling noises met his protest.

He ground his teeth. "I have a meeting Thursday morning."

It was nothing but the truth. Thursdays were meeting day. And if he didn't have one with someone from an agency or a supplier, he and Suzette spent the time discussing on-going developments at the Moonstone and the other inns he'd bought over the past year. It was right there on his appointment calendar. In ink.

Not that Fiona believed him.

"I have meetings every Thursday morning," Lachlan told her.

"Of course you do. I should have guessed." A tiny smile played on her lips. "I'll bet you have *lots* of meetings coming up. I'll bet your life is just *full* of meetings." Her singsong tone mocked him.

"Fine. I'll change the meeting," he snapped. "You want me nude, you'll get me nude, sweetheart. Thursday morning." He looked straight at her. "Six o'clock."

"Six o'clock!"

"What's the matter?" he asked smugly. "Too early for you? I thought you looked a little ragged." Deliberately he let his eyes rove over her mussed hair and unironed shorts. "Too bad. Some of us have jobs. Or maybe you'd like to change *your* mind?"

Fiona drew herself up sharply. "Six o'clock will be fine. I'll look forward to it."

"You do that." He went out the door and down the steps. "I'll see you then."

"I'll see *you* first!" Fiona's voice carried after him on a soft laugh.

"I SAW *The King of the Beach* this morning," Carin announced cheerfully when Fiona arrived at her shop that morning with a wheelbarrow full of sculptures. "I love the new arm. It gives him power. You ought to hang something on the end of it."

I did, Fiona thought as she unpacked the wheelbarrow and carried the sculptures into the shop. But saying so would have meant explaining what she'd hung there, which would have led to explaining why it wasn't there now, which would have led the conversation even further in a direction she didn't want to go.

Had she really told Lachlan McGillivray she wanted to sculpt him nude?

Had he really agreed to do it?

"But I guess you have to wait for something to wash up, don't you?" Carin went on.

"Yes." Fiona ducked outside to get more sculptures.

"You're at the mercy of the tide," Carin told her with a grin when Fiona came back.

Or her own idiocy. She hadn't been able to focus since Lachlan had stomped down her stairs and stalked away. What had she *done?*

"Oh, this is great!" Carin held up a metal surfer balanced on his board, riding the break of a wave, the whole thing cut from a single square foot of steel. "Absolutely perfect."

Fiona smiled. "Glad you like him."

The surfer was the first new cutout she'd made in well over a year. There wasn't much surfing on Pelican Cay. The waves were rarely large enough to attract surfing aficionados. But over on Eleuthera there were a few spots that drew surfers from all over the world.

"You ought to be doing new things," Carin said. "Stretching a bit. Spreading your wings. I worry about you."

"I'm fine," Fiona assured her, just as she'd been assuring everyone since her father's death. "You don't need to worry about me."

Carin didn't look convinced. "Well, the surfer is a step in the right direction. I like him. What else can you do?"

Fiona wondered what Carin would think if she said she was going to sculpt Lachlan McGillivray nude!

She was still in a state of panic every time she thought about it. Not just because of Lachlan. Because she didn't know the first thing about terra-cotta sculpting!

Not that it would matter, she assured herself, because it wouldn't happen.

But it had been worth it to see the look on Lachlan's hard handsome face.

Lachlan McGillivray had always been too high-and-mighty for his own good.

"What have you got against McGillivray?" her brother Paul had asked her when she'd begun the sculpture on the beach.

"Ride out a storm with him, I would," Paul had said. And Mike had agreed. "He's a good guy."

But Fiona couldn't see it.

As far as she was concerned Lachlan McGillivray was still a weasel.

He'd called her "carrots" from the moment he'd met her, when she'd been almost nine and he a haughty fifteen. *No one* called Fiona carrots! *Ever!*

Except Lachlan.

He'd even tugged her braid whenever she'd got close.

Not that he'd let her get anywhere near him. She and his sister Molly had spent a lot of hours trying to. They'd been studying to be secret agents in those days, lurking in the bushes, peering around corners, peeking over the rocks.

"Spying," Lachlan had accused furiously, "on me!"

Could anyone resist a challenge like that?

Well, Molly probably could have. She had to live with Lachlan, after all.

But Fiona had been inspired. And intrigued.

Despite his bad attitude toward the island—and toward her—there had always been something about Lachlan McGillivray...

Or something perverse about her own hormones, Fiona thought grimly. Because heaven help her, over the years her fascination with him had never waned.

She'd been besotted with him.

Lachlan, of course, had not been besotted with her.

He would be, she assured herself, once he realized she'd grown up. She remembered with total clarity and abject humiliation the day she'd decided it was time to make her move.

It had been the summer after Lachlan's graduation from high school. He was leaving in a few weeks to go to Virginia to university, and Fiona, nearly thirteen, entering puberty with a vengeance, had known time was running out.

If she wanted to convince Lachlan that there was someone worth coming back to on Pelican Cay, she had to hurry. She couldn't wait for her shape to get any curvier or her breasts to get any bigger. She wasn't quite stick-straight anymore, but voluptuous certainly wasn't her.

Still, the next time her father went to Nassau, she begged to go along, and while he was buying supplies, she'd gone to Bitsy's Bikinis and bought a suit she would never have dared buy on Pelican Cay. It was bright blue—what there was of it—and the fabric shimmered when it was wet.

"Like the sunlight sparkle on the sea," the saleslady told her. "You be smashing. Everybody notice you."

Not everybody.

The day she finally got up the guts to wear it, Fiona had lain on her towel on the sand right in front of where she knew he would come down to the beach even though there was a family of tourists camped right in front of her.

She'd gone early so she wouldn't miss him. And she'd slathered on sunscreen because she was cursed with her redhead's complexion. Then she'd arranged herself as enticingly and voluptuously as she could, and opened her book and pretended to read.

She'd waited. And waited.

The tourist family splashed in and out of the water and ran up and down the beach, and stayed cool. There were parents and two boys and a college-age girl. They started an impromptu volleyball game and invited her to join them.

But Fiona had shaken her head. There was no way she was going to jump up and down and jiggle in Bitsy's blue bikini. "No, thanks," she said politely and sweated and sweltered and waited.

Hugh came down with several of his friends. They ogled her and made comments. Hugh had whistled admiringly, and that teasing pain-in-the-butt Carson Sawyer had winked and suggested she go with him to the old shed behind the water tower.

Fiona flushed. "As if," she'd dismissed them. "Scram."

But she was glad the boys had noticed—even if their comments were completely immature. It gave her confidence.

So when Lachlan finally appeared on the rise overlooking the beach a little while later, she rolled oh-so-casually over on to her side and waited for him to see her.

He scanned the beach briefly, as if he were looking for someone. He shook his head at Hugh who had shouted something to him.

Then, as she'd known it would, his gaze came to rest on her.

"Hey!" he called eagerly.

Fiona smiled her best come-hither smile. She hadn't had a lot of practice in real life, but she'd worked on it in the mirror for weeks. And it must have worked, because Lachlan grinned broadly, then came sprinting down the trail.

Fiona sat up, a welcoming grin lighting her face.

And Lachlan hurtled right over her! "Stacie! Hey, Stace! I got my dorm assignment at UVA!"

The blonde girl looked over from the volleyball game with her brothers. "Oooh, cool, Lachlan! Which one? Maybe we'll see each other there."

And as Fiona watched, he showed her the letter. They looked at it together, their heads bent over it, so close her hair brushed his cheek. He touched her hand. She touched his arm.

Fiona sat there, stunned. He'd never even noticed her.

She should have left. Perversely, she couldn't seem to. Not yet.

Maybe she was a glutton for punishment. Maybe she just needed her teeth kicked in. But instead of running home, she lay back down on her towel, swallowing against the ache in her throat, and watched as Lachlan and the girl walked hand in hand down to the water. She watched them swim and splash each other.

She blinked back tears when, a while later, they came out of the water together and flopped down on the sand just yards from her, still talking and laughing and touching.

She really would be an excellent secret agent, she thought bitterly. She was absolutely invisible.

He never would have seen her at all if she hadn't heard him say how glad he was to be going, how much he longed to leave Pelican Cay.

It was the last straw. It didn't matter so much that he ignored her, but he was so wrong about the island! He was so wrong about everything!

Quite without thinking, Fiona jumped up and blurted, "So leave, then! Just get on a boat and get out of here!" She glared at him furiously.

Lachlan looked up, stunned. Stacie frowned. They both looked as startled as if a seashell had begun to speak!

"Go to hell, Lachlan McGillivray," she muttered under her breath, grabbing her towel and running away up the beach.

She'd had two more encounters with Lachlan since.

The New Year's before last he'd come to Pelican Cay to visit his brother. Fiona, who had heard through the island grapevine that he'd arrived with a couple of his teammates, had determinedly stayed out of his way.

It hadn't been hard. At that time she was spending most of her days and nights at home taking care of her father. She didn't go to the beach or frequent tourist spots except to do quick caricatures to sell to the tourists. She certainly wouldn't do one of him—though she'd done more than a few for her own enjoyment over the years.

She might have managed to avoid him altogether that time—if he'd been equally willing to avoid her.

She was surprised he hadn't been. And more astonished still when he'd come up to her in the Grouper that evening and invited her for a drink. She'd felt an odd, crazy desire to let bygones be bygones, to dare to say yes.

But then she'd seen his mates sitting at the bar, grinning and watching the two of them, and she understood that it was a joke. Why would a hunk like Lachlan bother with a woman like her—except as a joke?

"No," she'd said. It had hurt—but it had saved her worse pain down the road.

She didn't see him again for over a year. She didn't even know he'd come back last winter. But one afternoon she'd come in from taking some sculptures up to Carin's and her father had said Hugh needed her to go on a double date with him.

"With Hugh? Why?" She and Hugh were friends, but they'd never dated at all.

"Didn't say," her father told her. "Just said he wanted you. And I said you'd go."

"Dad!"

"Why not? You need a night out," he'd told her gruffly. Which might have been true.

But *not* with Lachlan McGillivray!

She'd been expecting Hugh. She'd been slack-jawed with disbelief—and panic—when she'd opened the door to find Lachlan standing there. "What are *you* doing here?" she began. Then she understood. "Oh, you must have come to see my dad—"

"No, I'm here for you."

"But—"

"Hugh is waiting at the restaurant with Deanna. You look fantastic," Lachlan said smoothly, taking her arm and leading her down the steps.

"But—" But she hadn't had time to get her defenses well in place, and while her brain might have been screaming no, her hormones were letting her be led.

Fool that she was, she'd let herself be led far too long that night—all the way through dinner with Hugh and some supermodel girl he was trying to impress, all the way along the beach where she and Lachlan had gone to walk and talk after, while Hugh had taken the supermodel heaven knew where.

To bed, no doubt.

Which was where Lachlan seemed to be heading with her!

He'd walked her back down the quay toward her place. But instead of taking her home, he'd said, "Come see the boat I bought."

And Fiona, who had been living in a dream all night, floating along on an evening right out of her childhood fantasies about herself and Lachlan McGillivray, opened her mouth to say no and found herself saying yes instead.

After all, it was still early. Not even close to midnight. She was still Cinderella at the ball. She didn't want to go back to her cold lonely reality just yet.

She could still feel the press of his hard warm fingers wrapped around hers as they'd walked down to the dock. She could still smell the salt air and the hint of lime in his aftershave as he helped her up and over the rail on to his new boat.

It was a brand-new sailboat, one she'd admired from a distance, wondering who it belonged to. Someday, she'd promised herself, she'd go out for a sail on a boat like that. The only boats she'd been on were the grimy smelly diesel-powered fishing boats her brothers used.

"It's lovely," Fiona had whispered, running a hand over the brightwork as they stood in the bow and the boat rocked under her feet.

"Not as lovely as you." Lachlan's voice had sounded a little ragged around the edges, its rustiness surprising her as much as the words.

Lovely. Lachlan thought she was lovely. He was touching her cheek, smiling at her. And just like in her dreams, he drew her against him and touched his lips to hers.

It was all there—everything she'd ever dreamed of—the taste, the heat, the passion.

And she couldn't help it. She gave herself to it. Her lips parted, and when his tongue sought entry, she met him hungrily. She was kissing Lachlan McGillivray.

Even better, *he* was kissing *her!*

And when he slid an arm around her and whispered, "Let's go somewhere more comfortable," she almost nodded, almost said yes.

She wanted it. She wanted him. But even more, she wanted forever.

And she knew that Lachlan didn't.

She might not have seen Lachlan McGillivray in person very often over the years. But it would have been hard to miss Lachlan in the tabloids. His hard handsome face was everywhere. He had the reputation of an athlete whose prowess on the pitch was only matched by his prowess between the sheets.

"It's exaggerated," Molly said. "The press makes it up."

But the press hadn't made up the red panties collection. And the sudden memory that she was actually wearing a pair of red panties that very evening had jolted her mid-kiss.

Dear God! He wouldn't!

And as she felt him start to draw her toward the cabin, she had wrapped her arms around him again, held on even more tightly, kissed him deeply one last time—then tipped them both right over the railing and into the harbor!

"Well, I'm delighted with your work," Carin was saying now. "Now if you'd just find a man."

"Carin!"

"Well, you're not getting any younger."

"And you are getting completely politically incorrect," Fiona retorted sharply. "I don't need a man."

"I didn't say 'need,' Carin soothed. "I just thought you might enjoy—"

"Well, stop thinking. I've got a man in my life."

"Oh?" Carin's eyes went wide. "Who?"

Fiona grinned. "He's about ten feet tall with arms made of driftwood and—"

Carin laughed, then shook her head. "Seriously, Fiona, Nathan has a photographer friend coming to stay next week. Nick's a really nice guy. Maybe he—"

"I'm not having you set me up on a blind date! I *hate* blind dates!"

Carin blinked at her vehemence. "Voice of experience?" she asked mildly.

"Yes! No." Fiona changed her tune rapidly. "I just think it's a bad idea. You can't rush these things. I'll find my own man when I'm ready."

"As long as you don't wait too long."

"Says the woman who waited thirteen years."

Carin gave a rueful laugh. "Some of us are a bit slow." She turned as the bell jangled and the door opened and a tall dark-haired man with a toddler on his shoulders came in. "But eventually we get it right. Don't we, Nate?" she smiled at the man.

"We got it right," Nathan Wolfe agreed and wrapped his wife in a hard one-armed hug while he held on to his son's feet with his other. Then he gave Carin a smacking kiss for good measure.

Fiona smiled at the sight. In fact Carin and Nathan did give her hope. She might have spent nearly ten years alone while taking care of her father. But Carin and Nathan had spent thirteen years apart before he'd discovered exactly why she'd jilted his brother at the altar—because she loved Nathan and was expecting his baby.

That baby, Lacey Campbell Wolfe, was now a very grown-up fourteen. Their son Joshua, born last year, grinned at her now and thumped on his father's head.

"Don't you think Fiona could use a good man?" Carin said to her husband.

"Carin!" Fiona protested.

But Nathan nodded. "Absolutely. Unfortunately I'm all out of brothers."

"Stop!" Fiona demanded.

"We're only trying to help." Carin looked aggrieved.

"I don't need any help," Fiona said firmly. "I'm doing just fine."

"I guess," Carin said, but she didn't look convinced. "At least you did a new sculpture," she said, showing the surfer to Nathan. "It's a start. You should do something else new this week."

"I will," Fiona promised.

"Great. I can hardly wait to see it."

Fiona smothered a grin. She could just imagine what Carin would say if she trundled in a sculpture of Lachlan McGillivray nude!

Wasn't going to happen. No way on earth.

He'd never ever do it.

He WAITED FOR HER to contact him, to tell him what she really wanted in exchange for removing her damned sculpture.

"Were there any messages?" he asked Suzette when he got back to the inn Monday night.

She glanced at her notes. "Dooley called about the roof on the Sandpiper. And the lumberyard called from Nassau."

"No one else?"

"Lord Grantham. He'll be arriving Wednesday night."

Lachlan drummed his fingers on the bookcase. He scowled out the window. There seemed to be new additions to Fiona's monstrosity. The "king" had an actual six-pack where his abs would be. He had a lasso dangling from his hand. And he seemed to be wearing a baseball cap.

Lachlan could just imagine the cultured Lord Grantham's reaction to that.

"Did Fiona Dunbar call?"

Suzette blinked and shook her head. "Was she supposed to?"

"No. No. I just thought she might."

She didn't call Tuesday afternoon or evening, either. Nor did she call Wednesday morning, though he was in his office the whole time, right there by the phone.

Lachlan felt sweat sliding down his spine and wondered if there was something wrong with the air-conditioning. He also wondered if she actually meant to go through with it.

That thought prompted a vague hollow feeling in the pit of his stomach. And feeling it made him furious. It wasn't as if it bothered him to take his clothes off, damn it!

He'd taken his clothes off lots of times, in front of lots of women. He wasn't any damn prude.

But he sure as hell had no intention of taking his clothes off in front of Fiona Dunbar so she could stare at him, ogle him, *judge* him!

He slammed his hand against the doorjamb.

Suzette looked up from her calendar, confused. "Did I get something wrong?"

"No. I'm just…thinking."

"About…?"

He shook his head. "Never mind." He raked a hand through his hair, agitated, needing a release, wanting to kick something—some*one!*

"I'm going for a swim!" he decided abruptly.

"But, Lachlan, we need to—"

"Let me know if anyone calls."

SHE THOUGHT HE WOULD CALL. She expected he would ring her up and give yet another excuse as to why he couldn't possibly be there on Thursday morning.

But he didn't call on Monday, and though she worked at the bakery on Tuesday morning and in Carin's shop on Tuesday afternoon, she did have an answering machine. And there were no messages on it.

So was he really going to show up?

Strip off his clothes?

Expect her to sculpt him?

Dear God.

She called Hugh and ordered the clay. She called her brother Paul to help her build a modeling stand and armature. She dragged out all her books on sculpture and began to read them feverishly.

He wouldn't show up, she assured herself.

But what if he did?

Would she dare to try to sculpt him?

LACHLAN LAY AWAKE all night Wednesday night. There was, he figured, always the chance that the world would end by Thursday morning.

If it did, he didn't want to miss it.

When it hadn't by five, he dragged himself out of bed with all the enthusiasm of a man told to set the alarm for his own execution. He got dressed, briefly debated on whether he ought to wear shorts or jeans for the occasion, then asked himself savagely what the hell difference it made.

Then he slipped quietly out of the inn, stood glaring into the darkness for one long minute in the direction of *The King of the Beach*. And then he turned and looked at the Moonstone—his future, the island's future.

"Life," his father had warned him when he was a boy, "isn't all fun and games. Sometimes you have to make sacrifices for what you want, for what you believe in."

And Lachlan had nodded gravely, ready to do his all.

Somehow he'd never imagined his "all" coming down to taking off his clothes for Fiona Dunbar.

At five forty-five he mounted her steps and tapped on her door. His palms were damp. He dried them on his shorts. His stomach was queasy. He ignored it. At the same time, he was aware that this all felt oddly familiar, much like the way he felt before a match.

It was nerves. A good thing, he reminded himself. Nerves got the adrenaline pumping. They moved the blood around.

On second thought, perhaps *not* a good thing. His blood

appeared to be moving in a southward direction. His body wasn't thinking of this as a sacrifice. His body was doing things he didn't want it to do at all.

The morning hadn't dawned yet. Only the faintest sliver of light had begun to line the horizon as he'd left the Moonstone. There had been no one else up in the inn when he'd let himself out, the guests enjoying a long lie-in. He'd heard the sounds of Maddie, the cook, and Tina, her daughter, just coming in as he'd slipped out the front.

It would have been faster to go through the kitchen, but he hadn't wanted them to wonder where he was going at that hour.

He didn't see anyone on his walk over the hill and down into the village. There was, naturally, a bit more activity at the harbor.

From Fiona's front porch overlooking the water, he could see a few small lights moving as fishermen preparing to leave, hauled nets on to the dock and into their boats. Some were already aboard, and the low rumble of the diesel engines began to fill the air.

Lachlan envied them. He'd gone out fishing a few times with the locals when he was a teenager. He'd even gone with Fiona's father and brothers, working alongside Mike and Paul, doing the grunt work, pulling his weight, but glad he didn't have to earn his living that way.

Now he stood with his back to Fiona's front door, watching and wishing he was going with them. Working his tail off hauling nets all day was a damn sight more appealing than what he was going to be doing.

Unless, he thought hopefully, she didn't answer the door.

If she didn't—if, he thought with marginally more cheerfulness, she slept right through their appointment—he could turn around and go back home again, obligation fulfilled.

It could happen. Fiona Dunbar was obviously not a morning person.

He knew he'd got her out of bed the day he'd come pounding on her door. He hadn't pounded today. He'd knocked lightly. No sense in waking the dead, he'd told himself. Or the neighborhood.

Or Fiona.

And then he heard a creak and the door behind him opened. Reluctantly Lachlan turned.

Fiona stood in the doorway, blinking raccoonishly. There were dark circles under her eyes. "You're here."

Was that disappointment in her tone? All she had to have done was tell him she'd changed her mind!

Or had she expected he'd wimp out?

Like hell.

"Six o'clock Thursday," he said gruffly. "Where else would I be?"

She shook her head. Managed a few more sleepy blinks. Damn, but he wished she would stop looking so beddable! That was the last thing he needed to think about bedding Fiona Dunbar right now.

Finally she'd blinked enough, and instead frowned accusingly at him. "You're early. It's not six."

"I could hardly wait," he said drily.

She looked momentarily nonplussed. Then she gave a jerky nod and pushed open the screen door. "Come in."

He followed her in. She was barefoot, wearing an oversize T-shirt and a pair of shorts, her long fiery hair hung loosely down her back. His fingers itched to reach out and touch it. He shoved them into the pockets of his trousers.

"So," he said, determinedly businesslike, "you got the clay?"

He knew she had. His brother Hugh had said so last night.

"What the hell does Fiona Dunbar need with a hundred pounds of clay?" Hugh had demanded when they'd been drinking beers at the Grouper.

Lachlan had nearly spat his own beer across the room. *"A hundred pounds?"* Good God.

Hugh had nodded, then shaken his head. "Wouldn't tell

me what it was for. Our little Fiona is getting mysterious in her old age."

Thank God she hadn't, was all Lachlan had been able to think. "Maybe she's going to make pots."

"Maybe." But Hugh hadn't looked convinced. "What would you do with a hundred pounds of clay?" he'd asked Lily, the barmaid.

Lily grinned. "Make me a man."

Then Lachlan had choked on his beer.

"Why not?" Lily had said with a shrug. "Better than the real ones be livin' 'round here."

"I've got the clay," Fiona told him now. "It's upstairs in my studio." She turned and briskly led the way.

Lachlan had been up these stairs as a teenager when he'd come home with Paul and Mike. They'd shared the bedroom at the back of the house under the eaves. Fiona's, he remembered, had been the tiny one across from the bathroom. And their parents' had been the wide room that sat above the living room and overlooked the harbor.

Lachlan imagined that Fiona would have moved in there and that she'd have turned her bedroom or the boys' into the studio. So he was surprised when she went straight to the large room that had been her parents'.

"I work in here," she said, opening the door. Then she stopped abruptly and nodded toward a door across the hall. "That's the bathroom. You can change in there."

She said the words so fast he almost missed them. And while he was still digesting them, she turned swiftly and vanished into her studio. The door banged shut after her.

Just like that.

Lachlan stood where he was and heard her words echo in his head.

You can change in there.

Change into what?

Nothing.

The moment of truth.

His pound of flesh. Literally.

Lachlan sucked in a slow careful breath. He stared at the closed studio door. Beyond it he heard the clatter of something being dropped, followed by Fiona's mutter of consternation.

The next breath came a little easier. If he was nervous, he reassured himself, so was Fiona.

Small consolation, though, he thought as he shut himself in the bathroom and fumbled to unbutton his shirt.

She wasn't going to be bare-assed in a matter of minutes.

BE CAREFUL WHAT YOU WISH FOR, Fiona's sainted dead mother used to say, for you will surely get it.

The warning hadn't had any urgency because Fiona had never been in danger of getting anything she'd wished for—until today. Now she stood in a stark white panic in the middle of her studio and wondered if it would help to breathe into a paper bag.

She hadn't believed he would come!

Her hands shook. *Stop it! Stop it! Stop it!* She jammed them into the pockets of her shorts, curled them into fists and willed them to be still.

How in God's name was she going to sculpt Lachlan McGillivray in the nude?

Whether he was naked or not, in the final analysis, had nothing to do with this. It was the sculpting that was the issue.

She'd make a complete fool of herself! She'd never sculpted anything—other than a few lumpy pelicans—in her life!

She didn't know how!

Had never been taught!

"You must do a thing before you know how, in order to know how after you have done it." She remembered her sixth grade teacher, Mrs. Cash, telling them that. "Plato said that."

Good old Plato.

"No time like the present," her father always said with

great good cheer whenever he'd encouraged his children to tackle some monumental task.

Good old Dad.

"Yes, well…" Fiona muttered, twisting her fingers together in anguish, because all at once the present was *now!*

"You," she said aloud to both Plato and her father, "have a lot to answer for."

As did her own big mouth.

She set the armature on to the modeling stand she'd begged Paul to build for her. Her fingers trembled as she fitted a paper cone over it on which to begin.

Charlatan! Imposter!

Stop!

She dug out a great lump of clay, thumped it on the work table and began desperately to knead it, press it, curl it, desperate to give her hands something to do.

It felt far diffcrent from the hard metal and shells she usually worked with. The clay was cool and damp under her fingers. It was pliable, responsive. Alive. Vital.

But nowhere near as alive and vital as the very naked man who that very moment strode into the room!

CHAPTER THREE

"RIGHT," Fiona said with the briskness of his college soccer coach on the first day of practice. She indicated a small homemade carpeted platform raised about a foot off the ground on the other side of the room. "You need to stand on here."

Lachlan stared at it. It was one thing to make a dramatic entrance. It was another to have to walk across the whole damn room.

Fiona smiled at him expectantly, just as if he weren't standing there completely starkers. God, but she had to be enjoying this!

"The platform?" Fiona said helpfully, as if he needed directions.

Lachlan's jaw tightened. Fine, let her have her moment of glee. He had nothing to be ashamed of!

Still, feeling totally exposed—which was exactly what he was—Lachlan did his best to look nonchalant, as if he paraded around naked all the time.

An early-morning breeze lifted the pale-blue curtains, blowing across his heated flesh, and wafting between his very bare thighs. It should have cooled him, settled him, calmed him.

Not quite.

He'd spent the past five minutes in Fiona's bathroom telling himself this was no big deal. It wasn't as if he'd never been naked in front of a woman before.

But they'd always been naked, too. And wanting him.

Fiona wasn't naked. And she didn't want him.

He just wished she did.

And thinking *that* was a really bad idea, because the very notion of Fiona Dunbar naked and desiring him nearly undid all his previous focusing on icebergs and multiplication tables and trying to do the square root of 842 in his head.

"That's right," she said and nudged the platform with her calf. "Come on up and get comfortable."

Get *comfortable?* He almost laughed as he crossed the room toward her.

But as he approached, Fiona moved across to her worktable where she had some metal gizmo sticking up out of a piece of wood. There was a slab of clay lying beside it. And she turned her attention to studiously laying scrapers and wires out on the table. As she did so, he felt slightly more at ease and stepped on to the platform.

It moved under his feet and he nearly lost his balance. "Cripes!"

"Oh, sorry." Fiona glanced up. "I should have warned you. Paul made it so it would turn. That way, as I work, neither of us has to move."

"I see." He was beginning to. And he wasn't liking what he saw. "Did you, er, tell Paul...what you were, um, going to do with it?" He could just imagine what Paul would have to say—forever—about that!

"Not specifically."

"Thank God for that," Lachlan muttered, steadying himself as the platform did another quarter turn again. Just what he needed—to be turned in a circle so Fiona could ogle him from every angle. Irritably he shifted from one foot to the other. "How am I supposed to stand?"

Fiona looked up. It was the first time she'd actually stared straight at him, scrutinized him—full-on—since he'd come into the room.

He went perfectly still—and wished he had some place to put his hands.

Her eyes roved slowly and consideringly over him. He

didn't move, except to clench his fists, grind his teeth, think of icebergs.

"Take your time," he muttered, feeling his whole body begin to burn.

"What?"

"Nothing. Just hurry up. I haven't got all day."

"Sorry. I've never done this before."

"Neither have I," he told her impatiently. "It's not rocket science, though."

"Fine. Just stand like that," Fiona said "Or maybe you could shift your weight a little to the right."

Lachlan shifted, trying to look at her, to see what she wanted, and *not* to look at her, because she was too damned attractive, at the same time.

"Not so much." She started to cross the room toward him.

Christ! She wasn't going to *touch* him, was she?

"Just tell me," Lachlan said through his teeth. *Icicles. Polar bears. Penguins walking single file and jumping into the Arctic Sea.*

Abruptly Fiona stopped. "It's all right. You're, um, fine."

Was she blushing? He hoped so. She deserved to be.

She backed hastily toward her worktable again. "And you're comfortable that way?"

Oh, yeah. "Just super."

If she recognized sarcasm when she heard it, she gave no indication. She reached into the drawer in her worktable and pulled out a pad of paper.

Lachlan frowned. "What's that for?"

"I need to make sketches."

"The hell you do." Modeling naked was bad enough. He wasn't having sketches floating around! "No sketches," he said flatly.

"But—"

"Sculpting. You said sculpting. Not sketching." He glared at her. "So sculpt."

Fiona opened her mouth as if she might argue. Then her gaze slid from his eyes all the way down his taut hard body—and back up again.

Lachlan steeled himself not to move, only to glare.

Her expression shuttered. But finally she shoved the sketch pad back into the drawer and shrugged. "Fine. No sketches."

Lachlan breathed again. He shifted back into a reasonable semblance of his earlier pose, the "comfortable" one. "This okay?" *Got a good view of everything?*

Fiona flicked a glance his way. "Yes. Um, sure." She gave him a vague fleeting smile. "I'll...just get started."

"Do that," Lachlan said grimly. And he shut his eyes and thought of Antarctica.

OH HELP.

Oh help, oh help, oh help.

It was the only mantra Fiona could think of, a prayer of desperation to a God who couldn't be blamed for thinking she deserved everything that was happening to her.

Here she was, with the most gorgeous naked man in the world standing just a foot away from her, and she could look, not touch. And, by the way, she was supposed to make a sculpture that would do justice to his body.

Impossible. There was no way. Fiona knew that.

But she had to do something. She couldn't just throw up her hands now and say, *I was only kidding. This is all a mistake. I can't sculpt.*

However true it might be, she couldn't say it.

Not to Lachlan McGillivray.

Because she had dared him—and he had accepted her challenge. Had *met* her challenge. And in doing so he had turned the challenge around on her.

Fiona wet her lips and raised her eyes to look at him—and couldn't look away again.

He had his eyes closed, thank God, which made it easier

to look. But looking just made her want more. She wanted to move closer, to walk around him, to reach out and touch.

A desperate sound choked in the back of her throat.

Lachlan's eyes snapped open. "What?" he demanded.

Dumbly Fiona shook her head. "N-nothing. Nothing at all!"

She ducked her head and grabbed the slab of clay and began shaping it around the paper cone that she'd put on the armature Paul had made for her. Determinedly she focused on it. She pressed it and wrapped it and smoothed it into something vaguely resembling a torso. Yes, like that. Not bad. It was a start. She took more clay and began to shape his legs.

They weren't going to be full-length legs.

The one book she had on clay sculpture, which she had studied in desperation last night in case he actually turned up, contained a step-by-step guide to sculpting a torso from midthigh on up. Obviously the author didn't think beginners ought to get bogged down in knees and feet.

"Stick to the basics," he'd written. "Focus on the essentials."

Fiona's gaze flicked up to focus on Lachlan's "essentials."

The tiny desperate noise threatened to choke her again. She hadn't seen a lot of naked men in her life. She'd cared for her father, of course, during his illness. But she didn't need to be Michelangelo to see that there was little resemblance between her ill, emaciated father and Lachlan McGillivray in his prime.

At thirty-five, Lachlan McGillivray was broad-shouldered and lean-hipped, all planes and angles and hard ropy muscles and tanned hair-roughened skin.

Mostly tanned skin, anyway.

So he didn't sunbathe in the nude? Somehow that surprised her.

Stop thinking about it. Stop thinking about him! she commanded herself. *Focus on the form. Concentrate.*

But focusing on the form didn't help. It brought her right back to the man. It was like telling herself not to think about pink elephants. Especially when the pink elephant in question was standing barely ten feet away.

So she looked. She couldn't help but look.

And as she did so, her fingers began to move.

Almost instinctively they worked the clay. She formed his thighs, pressing and shaping, pinching and smoothing. Then she moved on, creating the rough lines of his torso, his shoulders, his spine, his buttocks. Heaven help her, yes, even those!

God, he was glorious. She'd seen him on the soccer pitch, his movements quick and graceful, strong and fierce. And as she worked, her fingers seemed to give form and life to a body that could move like that. As she worked, pushing and pulling and coiling the clay, the fever in her brain seemed to ease. Her emotions quieted.

Yes, she thought. Oh, yes. From her eyes to her hands, everything seemed to flow. It was amazing, really, the feeling of the man taking shape beneath her fingers. It was completely different from anything she'd felt before.

Her cutout metal sculptures had always exuded energy. Inherent in the tension of the metal there was a sense of movement, a thrust that came from the flow of curve and line, a springiness that came from their form. They were the essence of action. They surfed, they fished, they swam, they danced.

Clay breathed.

It had substance, beyond its essence. It had solidity, strength and power. And as she worked it, as the sculpture began to take shape beneath her hands, Fiona began to understand how all those creation myths could say that humanity was created from the earth.

Now, as her sculpture came to life beneath her hands, she believed.

TIME WAS RELATIVE.

It flew—just like the cliché said it did—when you were having fun.

It moved with the speed of a glacier when you were standing stock-still and totally starkers under the scrutiny of the world's most irritating woman—a woman who unfortunately made your body sit up and take notice.

When they began, his body seemed intent on doing exactly that. So Lachlan thought all his coldest thoughts. He ran through polar bears and penguins, igloos and ice caps. He multiplied numbers and factored fractions and declined every German noun he knew.

And all the while he did it, he gritted his teeth and stared out the window or shut his eyes and waited for the session to be over.

She'd had her fun. She'd got an eyeful. He hoped she was satisfied.

He shifted slightly, irritably, and wished he had his watch on. His position might have been "comfortable" to start with. But even the easiest pose got wearying if you were stuck in it. He could hear her thumping and slapping the clay. How the hell long was she going to work?

He opened his eyes at last and ventured a quick glance Fiona's way, expecting to encounter a satisfied smirk.

But while she was staring straight at him, she didn't seem to be seeing him at all. Not the part he expected her to be focusing on, anyway. Her head was tipped to one side and she was scowling intently as her fingers stroked and shaped.

What she was stroking and shaping didn't look very promising to him—like the bottom half of some gangly loopy figure with a couple of iron prongs stuck in its butt. Maybe he was going to turn into a Picasso sculpture.

Whatever he was going to turn into, Fiona was totally focused on what she was doing. Her lower lip was caught between her teeth as she worked on the slope of his shoulder. She was joining something that might be an arm, scowling at it, then glancing at him, then back at the clay.

Intrigued by her focus and her intensity, Lachlan kept watching her.

Turnabout was fair play after all. No reason why she should get to do all the staring. And seeing Fiona Dunbar so serious, so focused on her work was something he hadn't expected at all.

"When did you start sculpting?" he asked abruptly.

She jerked at the sound of his voice and dropped the piece she'd been attempting to attach. Fumbling for it, she spared him only a brief glance as she began reattaching it. "I haven't. Much."

"Of course you have. The stuff in Carin's shop... The thing on the beach?"

She shrugged. "I've always done that."

"Did you take art in school?"

She shook her head.

"Why not?"

"They didn't offer it," she said irritably. "You know that."

"Here, I know. But after high school—"

"There wasn't any after," she said flatly. She focused on the sculpture, a line between her brows as she concentrated, and he thought she might not say any more. But finally she went on. "I thought about going to art school," she admitted at last. "But it wasn't that easy. We didn't have enough money to pay my way."

"There are scholarships."

"They don't give scholarships on the basis of nothing! You need a portfolio. Something to show what you've done!"

He'd never thought of that. His own family had been in such different circumstances. They'd come from the States, both his parents with college educations. His father had been a physician. His mother had taught school. There had been enough money to see them on their way. More importantly, there had always been parental support that had encouraged him and Hugh and Molly to discover and follow their dreams.

And each in their own way, they'd done just that. They'd all found success elsewhere. And they'd all come back to Pelican Cay. But Fiona apparently hadn't been anywhere.

"So you're totally self-taught?" he ventured. He'd almost forgotten he was naked now, except for when the breeze touched his bare skin. Then he remembered. But really he was too busy thinking about her.

"I'm self-*teaching*," Fiona corrected as she smoothed the clay of one of the legs, studied his intently, then bit her lip as she concentrated on the shape she was molding.

The figure was beginning to come together now—a man sure enough, rough but recognizable.

"And you've never done this before? Never worked with clay?"

"Never. No time. No opportunity. I've always just used what I have. Sand. Shells. Driftwood. Steel drums."

"Trash." Lachlan grinned.

Fiona bristled, but only for a moment. Then she shrugged, then informed him loftily, "Some scholars call it environmental sculpture. They say it's maximizing the assets inherent in the local setting."

"Do they?" Lachlan smiled at her pompous quotation and egged her on. "What else do they say?"

He was surprised when she told him. She'd obviously done a fair amount of reading on the subject. At first the words came slowly, and he almost had to drag them out of her. But when he persisted, she answered more fully.

She told him about books she'd read, theories she'd learned. The "king of the beach" was more than just trash, he began to realize. More than simply having a go at him, though he wasn't ready to believe that hadn't been part of her motive.

Still her interest in sculpture was obvious. She might be self-taught, and she might have gaps in her education, but she was clearly far more knowledgeable about the subject than he would ever have guessed.

Once he got her going, she talked at length. It seemed to relax her. It sure as hell made it easier for him. She kept right on working as she talked. He was fascinated to watch the clay she was pushing and patting and slapping become more and more recognizable as a decidedly male form.

It was hard to say which of them was more startled to hear a cell phone ring.

"Not mine," Fiona said quickly. "I don't have one."

Then his, obviously. He reached for it in his pocket and realized he didn't have a pocket. Or trousers. Cripes.

Fiona seemed to realize it, too. She flushed suddenly and looked away. "I'll get it," she blurted and darted out of the room, returning moments later to thrust the phone at him with a clay-encrusted hand. "Sorry."

He punched the answer button. "McGillivray," he barked.

"Where on earth are you?" Suzette demanded.

"What? Why? Who wants to know?"

"Lord Grantham, I expect," Suzette said shortly. "Since you've kept him cooling his heels half an hour."

"Grantham? I thought you scheduled him for nine." He remembered her rattling on about it last night, asking if that was all right with him. He remembered saying it was fine, to do whatever she wanted. He'd been far too preoccupied with other things.

"I did schedule it for nine," Suzette informed him. "It's twenty past."

"Past *nine?*" Lachlan started to look at his watch and realized he wasn't wearing that either. "Hell!"

"Are you still in bed? I sent Maddie to knock on your door, but she said you didn't answer."

"No, I'm not still in bed! I'm…out. I'll be right there. Give me fifteen—no, twenty minutes. Show him around." He hung up and jumped off the platform. "I have to go."

"Of course," Fiona said hastily. "I didn't realize—"

Neither had he. He hurried into the bathroom and grabbed his clothes, yanked on his trousers, hastily buttoned his shirt.

He'd intended to be casually elegant for his meeting with Grantham, who was upper-class elegance personified. He was going to be casually scruffy—as well as late—instead.

Hell. Again. He stuffed his feet into his flip-flops, opened the door, and came face-to-face with Fiona.

"When can you come back?"

"Back?"

"I'm not done," she said, trotting after him as he ran down the stairs. "I'm just getting started." There was an energy to her voice he hadn't heard before.

"I didn't say I'd keep doing this," he protested.

"We made a deal. I take the sculpture down. You pose for me."

"I've kept my part of the bargain."

"You've started to keep it," Fiona corrected. "I'm not finished." She looked at him beseechingly.

He'd never been beseeched by Fiona Dunbar before.

"You promised," she reminded him. "And so did I," she went on fervently. "I'll go over right now and start taking down *The King of the Beach*."

"The hell you will!" The last thing he needed was her messing with the sculpture while he was showing Grantham around. "You can do it tonight—after dark. The way you put it up."

"All right. I will." Still she held his gaze, her big green eyes earnest and intent. "It was going well today," she told him after a moment, sounding almost surprised. "It really was."

"Yeah." He had seen that. But still— "I have work to do. I have a life," he told her. "You didn't tell me it was an ongoing commitment."

"It doesn't have to be. I can work from photos."

"No!" *God no!* "Absolutely no photos."

"Well, then—" Was that anguish in her eyes?

Cripes, why couldn't he say no to this woman?

"All right! Fine. Tomorrow morning. Six o'clock again. No, make it five-thirty." If they got as absorbed as they had today, they needed to start earlier.

Fiona opened her mouth and he knew she was going to argue. But then she nodded. "Okay. Whatever you say. Just be here, please. Five-thirty."

"WHERE ON EARTH have you been?" Suzette pounced the minute he came in the door, giving him—and his canvas trousers and loose cotton shirt—a steely disapproving glare.

"I had business." Lachlan would have attempted to brush past her into his office, but Suzette stood between him and the door.

"Must have been exciting business," she said sarcastically and reached out and began unbuttoning his shirt.

"What the—? What're you doing?" Lachlan demanded, grabbing at her hands.

She batted his away. "Putting you together apparently. Next time you're out on 'business,' when you get dressed again, try to get the buttons in the right holes."

Lachlan groaned and shut his eyes.

Deftly Suzette did them up, then patted his cheek. He jammed his shirttails into his trousers, then swiped a hand through his hair, straightened his shoulders and looked at her. "Okay now?"

"Let's just hope he thinks you're so confident of his approval that you don't mind appearing like you just rolled out of bed."

"I didn't just roll out of bed!"

"Not yours anyway," Suzette agreed. "I gave him a tour of the inn, offered him a newspaper and a cup of coffee. But he decided to explore a bit, he said. He's gone out to see the grounds."

"What grounds?"

"The beach."

"Oh, hell."

LACHLAN HAD ENVISIONED Lord David Grantham as a graying fiftyish chap in tweeds with a pipe. What he found when he'd made a mad dash down the stairs and out on to the sand was a blond man barely as old as himself, wearing khakis and a navy polo shirt, moving slowly around Fiona's sculpture, staring up at it from every angle, taking it all in.

Wouldn't you know?

Lachlan sucked in a quick sharp breath, pasted his best "charming the public" smile on his face, and strode out to do damage control.

"Sir David," he said cheerfully, offering his hand and hoping *Sir* was proper address and that he shouldn't have called the earl *My Lord.* "I'm Lachlan McGillivray. Sorry to have kept you waiting."

Lord David Grantham turned his gaze reluctantly away from Fiona's "king of the beach," and, with a cheerful grin, took Lachlan's proffered hand. "Very glad to meet you. And please, call me Dave."

Dave? The director of the most prestigious custom travel group in Britain? The earl of GranSomethingOrOther? The heir, Suzette had told him, to lands five times greater than all of Pelican Cay? Lachlan adjusted his thinking.

"Right. Dave," he agreed heartily after a long moment. "Sorry not to have been here when you arrived. I had some business to take care of in town."

"No problem. It gave me a chance to look around on my own. I always like to get acquainted with places myself. It's fine to have staff do the preliminary visits, winnow out the chaff, as it were. But from there, I've always found it best to have a firsthand look at the place, form my own impressions of the inn, the surroundings, the local cultural—" a swift flicking glance toward the "king" "—amenities."

Oh, Christ.

"It's not staying," Lachlan said quickly, knowing exactly what he was referring to. "It's leaving. Tonight. The sculptor is taking it down."

"Taking it *down?*"

"Absolutely. We were discussing it this morning. It was never meant to be permanent. It was an experiment. A challenge."

"It certainly is." Dave nodded emphatically. "You can't take it down. It's exactly the sort of thing we're looking for."

Lachlan did a double take. "What?"

David looked surprised at his astonishment. "Oh, absolutely. The people on my tours can see all the Van Goghs and Vermeers and Rembrandts they want in Europe. They can pop over to the Louvre or to El Prado for a weekend. They cut their teeth on Tuscany. They have all done the proverbial grand tour until they're bored to tears. They're hungry for new experiences, new sights. They want life, vibrancy—" he jerked his head toward *The King of the Beach* "—this."

Lachlan opened his mouth, and closed it again. His mind reeled. He tried to think. And then to speak. "I thought they wanted quiet elegance, the unspoiled out-island, the pristine pink sand, the sea and the silence."

"Of course. That goes without saying. But it helps to offer something more," Grantham nodded eagerly, blond hair flopping over his forehead. "Something challenging and new. There are any number of unspoilt, quiet, out of the way islands, you know."

Actually Lachlan didn't know anything of the sort. In his view unspoiled out-of-the-way islands like Pelican Cay were few and far between these days.

But you didn't argue with a man like David Grantham. So Lachlan held his peace and counted to a hundred while David went on waxing poetic about Fiona's damned king of the beach.

"You see, it's not just that they want to get away from it all," he wound down at last. "It's that they want to come *to* something. They aren't used to total silence. They want a full cultural experience.'' He waved an all-encompassing arm. ''The sun and the sea and the silence, yes. But Culture—with a capital *C*, too. This—'' he gestured toward the king ''—and that steel band down at that little local bar. What's it called? The Scooper?''

''The Grouper.''

''Yes, yes. The Grouper. Amelie—she's the scout who found Pelican Cay—says the band is wonderful, that there's a talented composer there as well.''

Lachlan nodded. ''Skip Sellers.''

''Exactly. Just what we want. I'll have to hear the band, of course, to be sure. But Amelie says it's brilliant. And the ambience of the island and the inn… I hear there are a couple of excellent restaurants, too.''

''Beaches. And the Sand Dollar.''

''Excellent. And she mentioned a shop that hangs local art that she liked very much, but she said she wasn't able to talk to the owner.''

''Carin Campbell Wolfe.''

Grantham's eyes widened. ''The Carin Campbell who does those wonderful island watercolors?''

''That's her.''

Grantham was looking almost orgasmic with delight. ''But she's wonderful! I caught a show of hers in New York last year. I thought Amelie said she was on a shooting expedition?''

''Shooting pictures,'' Lachlan explained. ''Her husband is a photographer. Nathan Wolfe.''

''Yes, that's right. He had some photos in the show. Nathan Wolfe! Brilliant!'' He rubbed his hands together. ''Oh, this is wonderful. I wonder if they'd be interested in doing lectures for our guests.''

''You could ask.''

''Of course. We'll have dinner. Tonight, all right? You and me, the Wolfes and the steel band leader. Oh, and the sculptor.''

''The…sculptor?'' Lachlan swallowed.

Grantham nodded eagerly. "I want to talk to him. Want to learn more about his vision."

"It's a her."

"A *woman?*"

"Why not a woman?" Lachlan scowled in annoyance.

"Well, I—" David shrugged, but he was looking at the sculpture with new eyes. He exhaled sharply. "It's rather…large…and, um, strong…for a woman."

"Fiona's not exactly a shrinking violet."

David laughed. "Obviously." He rubbed his hands together. "Wonderful." He was beaming now. "I do love a strong woman."

Lachlan didn't like the sound of that. "She's a busy woman, too," he said sharply.

"But not too busy to have dinner with us, I hope."

Lachlan hesitated, then shrugged. "I'll see what I can do."

FIONA HAD A TRAY OF BOWLS full of conch chowder in one hand and a basket of homemade rolls in the other, a full section of tables that were her responsibility behind her, and Nikki, the other waitress, muttering in her ear about what Kevin, her boyfriend, had said to her last night.

It was all a wonderful dizzy buzz which Fiona let roll right over her because she was too busy thinking about how fabulous it had been this morning working on her sculpture. And all of a sudden she turned around, and Lachlan was standing in front of her.

"I need to talk to you."

"No!" She tried to spin away, aware that Nikki was looking at her, wide-eyed. Men like Lachlan McGillivray did not accost Fiona as a matter of course. Two tables of luncheon guests looked equally intrigued. "I'm working."

"Just for a minute," he persisted.

Fiona shook her head. She didn't want to talk to him. Didn't want to have him tell her he'd changed his mind, that he wasn't coming back tomorrow. This morning had been incredible. It had been perfect. She'd been terrified of making a fool of herself—of falling on her face, of gawking at him.

And, well, maybe she had gawked just a little.

But somehow—just how she didn't even know—it had quickly become more than that. She could sculpt! She could bring an image to life with her hands. It was so incredible, so empowering, she couldn't believe it.

She'd worked for over three hours. She'd made him stand there that long—far too long, she knew. And yet she couldn't help it. Time had just flown past. And even after he'd left, she had continued to work.

She had studied the torso, had felt it with her fingers, pushing here, shaping there, finding hints of the ridges and hollows and pads of muscle. She had closed her eyes and had seen Lachlan in her mind and she'd shaped and pushed and let her fingers move. Her whole body had hummed with an energy she'd never felt before.

She could hardly wait until tomorrow.

And she didn't want to hear his second thoughts, his excuses, why he couldn't come!

"Excuse me." She tried to step around him. He stepped in front of her. She moved the other way. So did he. Oh, for heaven's sake!

"I have a proposition for you," Lachlan said firmly, not giving ground.

"A proposition?" Nikki echoed, blinking owlishly, looking from Fiona to Lachlan, all avid interest. The table of customers right next to them gave up all pretense of trying to eat.

"Lachlan! For heaven's sakes! I'm *working!* Are you blind? Do you not see the tray? The food?" Fiona glanced over his shoulder, nodding at the table she'd been heading toward. "The starving patrons?"

Lachlan glanced over his shoulder, too, then turned and snatched the basket of rolls out of her hand. "Here you go.'' He passed the basket to the lady at the head of the table.

Fiona tried to stop him, but he elbowed her aside and unloaded all her bowls of chowder, plopping them down one at a time in front of each diner. Then he dusted his hands briskly together.

"There now. All set. Get you anything else?" He gave them a bright smile.

Negative shakes of heads and bemused looks all around.

Lachlan beamed and winked at them. "Then I know you won't mind if I borrow your waitress for a few minutes." He grabbed her hand. "If you need anything, just shout." And he dragged her out on to the street.

"Lachlan! Stop it. My boss will kill me. What do you think you're doing?" She tried unsuccessfully to snatch her hand out of his.

"Inviting you to dinner," he told her. "And making sure you accept."

Inviting her to dinner? This didn't have to do with tomorrow? "Dinner? When? Why?" she asked suspiciously.

"That meeting I had this morning, the one I was late for—" his mouth twisted "—was with Sir David Grantham, the head of—"

"Grantham Cultural Tours."

"You know him?"

"I know *of* him. Everyone knows *of* him," Fiona said. "Carin was talking about him. He's like a god in the high-end tourist industry." She paused, considering the implications of that. "David Grantham wants to bring his holidays here?"

Lachlan nodded. "I hope so. He thinks Pelican Cay has a lot to offer his clients."

Fiona doubted that. Grantham was far too Cultural—with a capital *C*—for a place like Pelican Cay. Grantham Tours took in-depth historical and artistic jaunts. "Why would they come here? What do we have? A rusty cannon? A straw shop? A conch bar?"

"All of the above," Lachlan agreed. "And the steel band and Carin's paintings and Nathan's photos. And—" he paused and did a mimed drum roll with his fingers "—*The King of the Beach.*"

Fiona flushed at his mockery. "I told you I'd start taking it down. You're the one who said to wait until tonight."

"You can't take it down. He loves it."

She stared at him. "Get out of here."

Lachlan raised his hands, palms out, as if fending her off. "God's truth," he swore. He was laughing at her.

Fiona bared her teeth. "And if I believe that, you've got a bridge to the mainland to sell me!"

Still grinning, Lachlan challenged her. "Come to dinner and he'll tell you himself. He wants to meet you."

"I don't believe you."

Lachlan shrugged. "Your loss." And just like that, he turned and started to walk away.

Fiona glared after him, furious. "Lachlan!"

He looked back, a grin flashing briefly as he cocked his head. "Yes, carrots?"

She practically squeaked with frustration. "Leave my hair out of this!"

"Whatever you say." He stopped laughing, but he didn't stop smiling at her. And the way he was looking at her turned her flush into a full-scale burn.

She didn't want him smiling at her! She didn't like the way it made her heart kick over, didn't like the way it made her insides all warm and wiggly. "Stop it," she muttered.

He shook his head. "Come to dinner, Fiona," he said quietly.

"I—"

"Seven-thirty. At Beaches with Lord Grantham, Carin and Nathan, Skip Sellers and his wife."

"I don't—"

"You want to sculpt, don't you? You want challenges, isn't that what you said?"

"Yes, but—"

"And you want to be able to leave that damned king of yours on the beach to charm and educate the tourists, don't you?"

She couldn't speak. She stared at him dumbly. "Not...not if it means you won't come tomorrow. It's good," she said desperately. "Not the king. My sculpture. The one of...you." She gulped. "It is. I know it is. I didn't know when we started. I was afraid...but now I need to keep going. It...feels right. So I've got to finish it."

For a long moment he just looked at her. Then he shook his head. "I'll come," he told her.

"But you said—"

"I'll come," he promised gruffly.

It felt as if the sun had come out. "Really? Honest?"

He jammed his hands in his pockets. "I said I would, didn't I? Tomorrow morning. Five-thirty."

She nodded eagerly.

"Only if you come to dinner tonight," he told her implacably. "Seven-thirty, Fiona. I'll pick you up."

CHAPTER FOUR

"I'LL COME," Hugh said cheerfully. He popped the top on the beer he'd just taken from his refrigerator and took a long draught from the bottle. "Always ready for a free meal."

"You're not invited." Lachlan grabbed a beer for himself since Hugh didn't offer any. "I only came to see if I'd left my navy blazer here." The last time he'd worn it, he'd been staying in the spare bedroom of Hugh's small beach house while he'd been working on the Moonstone. "The numbers are even the way they are."

"Numbers?" Hugh's brows hiked beneath a fringe of shaggy dark hair. A grin touched the corners of his mouth. "Is that, like, an etiquette thing?" He perched on the countertop next to the sink, swinging his bare tanned legs, holding the beer with one hand and reaching down to scratch his mutt, Belle, on the ears.

"It's like an etiquette thing," Lachlan agreed drily. "And since you don't do etiquette these days..."

Eight years of spit and polish in the U.S. Navy had been all the rules and regimentation Hugh had been able to tolerate. Since his discharge four years ago, he'd been turning casualness into an art form.

"I'm polite," Hugh protested.

"Besides," Lachlan went on briskly, rummaging through the coat closet, "Grantham already met you."

Hugh had flown him in from Nassau Wednesday afternoon along with Fiona's hundred pounds of clay. "The idea

is for him to get to know people on the island he might
want his tours to meet.''

"Like who?''

"Artsy types. Carin and Nathan. Grantham's with
Nathan now.'' Lachlan had taken him to visit Carin's shop
before he'd gone to see Fiona at the bakery. Nathan had
been going to pick him up there and give him a tour of the
island's photographic possibilities. "Skip and Nadine
Sellers.'' Skip was the lead singer and composer for the
local steel band Grantham had mentioned. "Fiona.''

Hugh stared, his beer halfway to his lips. "Fiona?
Dunbar?''

"That's right.'' Lachlan turned away and opened the
door to the broom closet. There were swim fins and a snor-
kel, an old fishing net and float he'd snagged years ago, a
couple of diving tanks, a string of pink flamingo patio
lights, and a couple of Hawaiian shirts. No blazer.

"Why Fiona?'' Hugh asked.

"She sculpts.''

"Well, yeah, but—''

"She *sculpts,*'' Lachlan repeated, unaccountably annoyed at Hugh's less than enthusiastic agreement.

Now, though, his brother was looking at him narrowly.
"Don't mess up Fiona.''

Lachlan banged the closet door shut. "What the hell do
you mean by that?''

"You took her to Beaches before,'' Hugh reminded him,
in case he'd forgotten.

"So?''

"So, the evening didn't end well. I seem to remember
that she made it pretty clear she didn't want anything to do
with you. Tried to drown you, didn't she?'' Hugh flashed
a quick hard grin.

Lachlan's jaw set. "Her foot slipped.''

At least that was what she'd told Maurice when he'd
fished them out.

"Uh-huh.'' Which meant Hugh wasn't going to argue

about it, but he didn't believe it either. He was looking unaccountably serious for a man who never got ruffled. His grip on the beer bottle was turning his knuckles white. "I don't know what you're thinking about Fiona, Lachlan, but you'd damned well better not hurt her."

"I don't plan to 'hurt' her. I plan to have dinner with her. And since when do you worry about Fiona Dunbar?" he demanded.

"Since her old man died and she's on her own."

"She's a grown woman."

"She hasn't been anywhere or done anything. She's an innocent."

"Not that innocent," Lachlan muttered under his breath, squatting down to rummage through one of the piles of laundry on the floor.

"What?" Hugh said sharply.

"Never mind." Did Hugh never put anything away? There were two heaps of clothes on the floor. The only difference seemed to be that one pile was grimier than the other. That must be how he told them apart. "You don't have to worry about Fiona," Lachlan said, burrowing to the bottom of each. There was no blazer in either of them. He sighed and stood up again. "As you so aptly pointed out, she can take care of herself."

"Just make sure she doesn't have to."

Their gazes met. Their eyes locked.

"It's dinner, Hugh," Lachlan said with a tight smile.

Hugh didn't smile in return. "As long as that's all it is."

Belle, clearly sensing the tension, whined and nudged Hugh's knee.

"Ah, right," Hugh said, breaking their locked gaze and rubbing the dog's ears once more. "Dinnertime." He slid off the counter.

Lachlan glanced at his watch. Hell. The dog was right. It was nearly seven already.

"And I'm going to be late." He kicked the rest of the

laundry out of the way as he headed for the door. "Don't you ever put anything away?"

"I keep things where I can find 'em," Hugh told him, unfazed as he reached for the kibble and the dog bowl. He waited until Lachlan was outside before calling after him, "I think your blazer's in the dog bed on the porch."

IT WASN'T A DATE.

Definitely not a date, Fiona told her underwear-clad reflection in the mirror.

And thank God for that. If Lachlan had asked her out—on a date—she'd have said no. No way. Never again!

But this wasn't a date. It was business.

And that was almost scarier.

That she should be having dinner with Lord David Grantham of the posh upscale Grantham Cultural Tours and an award-winning photographer like Nathan and a stunning painter like Carin (even though they were friends of hers) and who knew who else—*besides* Lachlan—was enough to make her stomach do what it had done when Hugh had taken her up in his plane and done a loop.

What did she know about the tourism business? Or the art business, for that matter?

Just this morning she'd been afraid she was out of her depth trying to do a terra-cotta sculpture. And while she felt better about her ability to do that now, it hardly gave her the credentials to hobnob with an earl!

She didn't know how to dress to hobnob with an earl. She wished she could talk to Carin. Carin would know how she should dress, how she should act, what she should say. Carin was sharp and sophisticated. She might have lived on the island for years, but she'd grown up in the city. She knew that sort of thing.

But when Fiona had got off work and run to Carin's shop, Elaine said cheerfully, "She gone home. Gotta make herself beautiful."

Which didn't exactly inspire confidence as Carin was already the most beautiful woman Fiona knew.

"Maybe I shouldn't go," she said to Sparks who, having finished his own dinner, was sitting on her dresser washing his paws and watching her rifling through her closet in vain. "I don't have anything to wear. There is nothing—*nothing!*—here!"

If she had expected him suddenly to turn into one of those cartoon animals like the ones who had whipped up Cinderella's ball dress, she was sorely disappointed. He stopped washing long enough to yawn. Then he turned around three times, made himself comfortable on her one good silk blouse, and went to sleep.

She snatched it out from under him. "Fat lot of help you are."

Well, the silk blouse was out. Covered with cat hair. And she only had two dresses: the one she'd worn to dinner the last time Lachlan had taken her to Beaches—not a memory she wanted to inspire—and the one she'd worn to her father's funeral. Also not an option.

"What am I going to do?" she demanded.

Sparks didn't even bother to purr in reply. Clearly he wasn't best pleased having his cushion snatched away from him.

Downstairs the front door rattled. Dear God, Lachlan couldn't be here yet, could he? She scrambled for her watch. Oh, whew. It was only just past six.

"Fee? Anybody home?"

Fiona breathed a sigh of relief. "Up here!" she called, relieved to hear her sister-in-law, Julie.

There was a bit of movement below, the sound of the refrigerator opening and closing, which opened Sparks's eyes briefly. Then there came the sound of elephants climbing the stairs.

Ordinarily Julie bore no resemblance to an elephant at all. But now, seven months pregnant with twins and—forget the elophant—big as a cruise ship, she finally gasped into view.

"Brought you some grouper," she said between gasps. "Fresh off the boat. I put it in the fridge so Himself—" a look based on prior experience passed between her and Sparks "—doesn't think it's for him. What's wrong? Are you sick? Why are you standing here in your underwear?"

"I'm supposed to be going out to dinner," Fiona waved a helpless hand toward her closet. "But I've got nothing to wear."

Julie's eyes got wide as it was a Rare Event for Fiona to go out at all. "Dinner? With who?"

"Lots of people. It's business."

"Paul didn't say anything about dinner out." As far as Julie was concerned, there was only one business—the fishing business. And Fiona did own a share of their boat as her legacy from her father.

"Not fishing," Fiona said. "Sculpting. The stuff I do for Carin and the, um…*King of the Beach*."

"The big trash thing?" Julie looked enormously impressed. "The one you were having a go at Lachlan McGillivray with?"

Fiona didn't answer that. But it didn't matter because Julie had already moved on.

"How'd that happen?" There was nothing Julie enjoyed more than news. She plumped herself down on Fiona's bed and looked expectantly at her sister-in-law.

Dutifully Fiona mumbled something about the earl and his tour company and Carin and Nathan and, because she knew it would get out anyway since Pelican Cay had no secrets at all, Lachlan McGillivray.

Julie's eyes bugged. She hooted. "You and Lachlan! He'll roast you!"

"He's the one who asked me."

"Lachlan did? You're joking. You tried to drown him!"

God, was she never going to live that down? "I did not try to drown him! We fell in the harbor."

"Oh, right. Of course," Julie murmured. "How could I forget?" She smirked, then sobered. "You're probably the only girl who ever said no to him."

If she had managed to say no to him, they wouldn't have ended up in the water, Fiona thought ruefully. But she didn't tell Julie that. She just plucked at the clothes in her closet once more. Time was running out and her fairy godmother was nowhere to be seen.

"I should just call and cancel."

"No, you shouldn't." Julie was adamant. "You have to go."

"I don't *have to,*" Fiona said.

"Yes you do. You need to get out. You hardly ever went out anywhere while you were taking care of Tom. It's time you had a social life. You need to meet people. How old is this earl?"

"What? Stop that!" Fiona exclaimed, realizing where her sister-in-law's thoughts were headed. "It's business, Julie!"

"Whatever." Julie didn't care. She was going full-speed now. "I have the perfect dress for you."

"*You* do?" Fiona stared at her, nonplussed.

"I wasn't always as big as a minivan," Julie reminded her. "Once I wore a size eight, too. And I bought a fabulous dress when Paul and I were in Nassau on our anniversary last year. It will be perfect. I'll call him and he can bring it over."

Fiona opened her mouth to object, but Julie was already reaching for the phone.

"You'll love it. It's elegant," Julie said. "Understated. One of those less-is-more dresses. Cost the earth. You'll be gorgeous in it."

Fiona hesitated—but only for a moment. She had no choice, really. There was no way she could call Lachlan and beg off. *I'm sorry. I can't come. I don't have anything suitable to wear.*

How could she say that to a man who had dared to let her sculpt him *naked?*

"Call Paul," she said and sighed fatalistically.

Julie called. "He'll be right over. One thing," she said when she hung up. "This dress is dry clean only. Try not to fall in the water."

LACHLAN DIDN'T PUT ON ARMOR before he went to pick up Fiona, but he gave it some thought.

Inasmuch as his navy blazer had literally "gone to the dogs," he put on his best khaki trousers, a blue oxford cloth shirt, then stopped by Suzette's quarters to tell her to meet them at Beaches at 7:30. Then he put on mental armor and set off to Fiona's.

He expected they'd have a battle.

She hadn't looked all that keen on the dinner invitation. If he hadn't had the morning sculpture session to play as a trump card, she'd probably have refused.

He fully expected she would be elbow deep in clay or some other messy substance when he arrived, in the hope that he would leave without her.

Not a chance, sweetheart.

Fiona was coming to dinner tonight if he had to clean her up and make her presentable himself! Actually, he thought with a grin, that wouldn't be much of a hardship. And it would serve her right for dumping him in the water last time they'd had dinner together.

He was grinning in anticipation as he went up the steps and pounded on her door.

So it was a bit of a shock to have it opened promptly by a stunning redhead wearing an emerald-green silk dress who smiled brightly at him.

"Right on time," Fiona said cheerfully. "Let's go." And she pulled the door shut behind her and, without even looking his way, headed briskly down the steps.

Lachlan stared after her, feeling gut-punched.

Where the hell had she got a dress like that? And what

was it Hugh had said about Fiona Dunbar being an innocent?

No innocent had ever worn a dress like that one! It was cut low in the back and displayed acres of gorgeous golden freckled skin. The dress nipped in at the waist and flared at the hips, swinging lightly around her legs as she walked. Two thin straps were all that held it up in front, and it didn't take a genius to figure out that she wasn't wearing a bra. Lachlan sucked air. It made his mouth dry just watching her. So much for cleaning her up and making her presentable.

He vaulted down the steps and hurried after her.

"Change of heart?" he drawled as he caught up with her near the straw shop. He tried to breathe normally.

She slanted him a glance. "What?"

"You didn't want to come, as I recall," he said, dodging around three boys kicking a ball in the street and falling into step beside her.

Fiona shrugged. "I decided I'd like to meet a real live lord."

He frowned at that, undecided if she was joking. He'd never thought Fiona Dunbar would be impressed by a title. But then he'd never thought Fiona Dunbar would own a dress like that either.

"Maybe you can sculpt him," Lachlan said.

Fiona smiled. "Now there's a thought."

"You'd better not suggest it," he said quickly in case she thought he was serious. "We want him to come here. For that matter I'd just as soon you didn't mention our, um…your, um, sculpting to anyone."

"Really? Why?" Fiona said guilelessly. Then, before he could reply, she burst out laughing. "I won't be telling anyone, believe me. It's our secret." She glanced up toward the top of the hill. "Look. There're Nathan and Carin. Is that Lord Grantham with them?"

Lachlan saw three people turning into Pineapple Street. "Yes."

"Ah." It sounded like a sigh of appreciation.

Lachlan gave her a narrow look. "What's that mean?"

"He's very nice." Fiona grinned. "Very nice indeed. Julie will be pleased."

"Huh?"

But Fiona just shook her head. "Nothing."

What was it with women, anyway? Couldn't they just say what they meant?

What it meant, he began to discover, was that Fiona liked David Grantham. And the feeling seemed to be mutual.

Lachlan had barely introduced them—"Fiona, David, Lord Grantham. Dave, this is Fiona"—and they were talking like old friends.

"Fantastic piece of art on the beach," Grantham enthused, taking Fiona's hand as if he had a right to it. "Don't you think so?" he said to Lachlan.

"Memorable," Lachlan said, refusing to look into Fiona's laughing eyes.

"Absolutely," Grantham went on, taking her by the arm and drawing her with him as he followed Carin and Nathan up the steps toward the restaurant. "It's incredible the way you've used just whatever came to hand. Everything that came in on the tide, is that right?"

"Almost everything," Lachlan heard her reply. "Although there was a bit of censorship at one point."

"Censorship?" Grantham looked askance.

"What censorship?" Nathan demanded.

"You never told me about that," Carin said to Fiona.

"Well, I—"

Lachlan intervened, pushing past them to grab the door, pulling it open and holding it for them all to go in. "There are some things that float in on the tide," he said firmly, "that are best not displayed in a public forum."

"Oh," Carin said. Her cheeks colored. "Of course. I never thought..." She gave him an embarrassed smile and hurried past him into the restaurant. Nathan followed, and Grantham with Fiona.

"And there are other things which could be and aren't," Fiona murmured for his ears alone as she sashayed past.

"Well, I say it's marvelous," Grantham said heartily. "Eye-catching. We'll feature it on the tour brochure."

"Feature it?" Fiona stared.

Lachlan's teeth came together.

"Why not? It's perfect," Grantham went on. "A set piece. Completely unique—exactly like a Grantham tour." He grinned at them both. "Come," he said to Fiona, "let's have a drink and you can tell me all about your work."

And she did.

At least Lachlan hoped that's what she was doing over the clatter of glasses and the soft calypso beat of the island version of Muzak.

He knew damned well what Grantham was doing. He was coming on to Fiona!

Lachlan caught a part of the questions Grantham asked about her inspiration while they had drinks. Far from being reticent in the presence of titled aristocracy, Fiona chatted easily with him. When Lachlan would have steered him away to talk to Skip and Nadine Sellers, he'd got brushed off.

"Later," Grantham promised. "I want to know more about what Fiona thinks of American Indian artists."

"American Indian artists?" Lachlan muttered into his beer. "What the hell does that have to do with anything?"

"They're getting to know each other. And she's charming him." Suzette answered his rhetorical question with more honesty than he needed. "You didn't need me here after all."

He'd asked her to partner Grantham. He'd expected to put Fiona next to him at the table, to make her feel comfortable, less out of her depth.

Instead he got to watch as Grantham brushed a strand of hair from her cheek as they talked over the conch chowder. And he got to see her blush over the box fish stuffed with sea grapes and rice when Grantham waxed eloquent about the brilliance of her sculpture—not just the monstrosity on the sand, but all the other pieces in Carin's shop.

"I don't know why you're staying here." Grantham's voice carried the length of their table even though he was speaking to Fiona. "Your work is wonderful. Universal. You could take it anywhere. The metal pieces have such movement. Such energy. And the pelicans and sand castles. They're pure unadulterated folk art," he claimed. "Innocent. Unspoiled."

"Like Grandma Moses," Lachlan said through his teeth.

Everyone's gaze turned to him. Nathan opened his mouth…and closed it again. Carin blinked. The Sellerses exchanged glances. Suzette stared. With a hard look Lachlan defied them to disagree.

"What a lovely compliment," Fiona said brightly after a moment of dead silence. "Thank you."

And then she went back to flirting with the earl.

Lachlan stabbed his bread roll and crumbled it into little pieces. The courses came and went. The chatter went on. Nathan and Skip talked about Nathan shooting some film of the steel band. Nadine and Carin compared notes about toddlers. Suzette even offered an opinion as she had a niece that age. At the far end of the table Fiona and Grantham went on talking to each other.

You'd have thought they were at a table for two!

Lachlan glared at them.

"Isn't it great?" Carin said cheerfully. She was sitting next to him, but she, too, was looking down the table at Fiona who was simpering at Lord Bloody Grantham.

Obviously he'd missed something. "Isn't what great?" he growled.

"Fiona. Flirting."

He turned his head and stared at Carin.

"We were worried she wouldn't remember how." Carin grinned. "It's been a lot of years. It's lovely to see that she is getting out, socializing, practicing her wiles…"

Now he turned back to look at Fiona. She tipped her

head back and laughed delightedly at something Grantham
was saying.

Was that what she was doing? Practicing her wiles on
Grantham?

Like hell.

FLIRTING, FIONA DISCOVERED, was like riding a bicycle.
She might be a little rusty, she might wobble at first, but
she hadn't forgotten how to do it.

And with a handsome, cooperative male like David
Grantham encouraging her—doing a fair bit of flirting on
his own—it wasn't long before she was pedaling right
along, laughing and talking, batting her lashes and doing a
bit of gentle teasing.

And thank God for that.

It kept her from staring down the table at Lachlan
McGillivray.

She needed a distraction. Every time she did glance his
way, his clothes seemed to fall off and she would see him
as she had seen him that morning—in all his powerful naked male splendor. It made her dry-mouthed and damp-
palmed just to think about it.

So she didn't. Or tried not to.

Instead she threw herself eagerly into conversation with
David Grantham. She'd imagined that he would be a pompous, old, self-important stuffed shirt. To her surprise and
pleasure he was affable, young, easygoing and capable of
charming the socks off any female between the ages of nine
and ninety—in this case, her.

Fortunately David had managed the seating arrangement
so that she was next to him at the end of the table. She'd
thought that Lachlan would be at one end of the table and
Suzette, his assistant, would be at the other. But somehow
David had contrived to have her at the end so that she could
stare straight down the table at Lachlan. Turning to her
right and smiling at David was a far less stressful prospect.

Besides, Lord Grantham—"Dave," he corrected her the

first time she used his title—was as charming and easygoing as Lachlan was not.

Tall and lean, with blond floppy hair, Viking good looks and a muscular build, David Grantham would have made an excellent nude model himself. But the thought of David's no doubt glorious naked body didn't make Fiona's heart skip a beat at all.

Still, his jokes made her laugh, his flirtatious teasing made her feel like an attractive woman but not simply a sex object, and his genuine interest in *The King of the Beach* and her other sculptures made her feel as if she hadn't been just cranking out holiday souvenirs, but had actually accomplished something worthwhile.

Even Lachlan's throwaway comment about Grandma Moses couldn't diminish her pleasure.

But David's request over their last cup of coffee that she consider giving some talks to his tour groups flabbergasted her. They had moved from casual flirtation to earnest discussion of art, and she'd found herself espousing theories that sounded right but which surprised even her. His request surprised her even more.

"Me?" Fiona thought perhaps that Silas the bartender had put a little too much Irish in her Irish coffee. "But…I'm not a teacher. I'm not even a professional sculptor."

"Of course you are. You sell your work. That makes you a professional."

"I have no training."

"Neither did Grandma Moses." David grinned.

"I don't know…" Fiona said, glancing down the table toward where Lachlan seemed to be listening to Nathan, all the while glaring at her. "He might think I'm interloping."

David followed her gaze. "He has nothing to do with this. Or does he?" The question was quiet, but there was something intent in the way he turned his gaze on her. "Does he have a claim on you?"

"No," Fiona said hastily. "Of course not. I just—he's the one who invited me to come to dinner."

"*I* invited you to come to dinner," David said. "*I* wanted to talk to you."

"Oh."

Oh. So it hadn't been Lachlan's idea, after all. Of course. She should have realized that. Everyone here was someone David had wanted to talk to. Lachlan had just made the invitation.

"Of course," Fiona said, still smiling, but at the same time she felt oddly hollow and bereft.

"So we'll talk further," David said briskly. "How about if I get you a few tapes of other artists and artisans who have worked with my tours. Then you'll see how well you'd fit in."

She could tell he wasn't going to take no for an answer. Not yet anyway. And if privately she thought he was a little too optimistic, she couldn't argue unless she knew more, could she? "All right."

"Brilliant!" David leaned over impulsively and kissed her cheek.

"Check!" Lachlan's harsh voice as he called the waiter made Fiona jump.

And David pulled back, surprised. "But—"

But Lachlan was already halfway to his feet, snapping his fingers and beckoning their waiter.

"Time we got moving," he said briskly, glancing at his watch. "Skip and Nadine have to head over to the Grouper for the first set. Nine-thirty, you said?" He looked at Skip.

"Well, it's not cut in stone," Skip said. "We can—"

"We'll go now. No sense in keeping the crowd waiting," Lachlan said. "You said you wanted to hear them, right, Dave?"

"That's right." David was getting slowly to his feet now, too, and held out a hand to Fiona. "Fancy a little music before we head home?" he invited her.

Fiona smiled. "That would be lovely. I—"

"—don't think so," Lachlan said firmly. "Fiona's got some work to do."

She stared at him. Work? What work?

But Lachlan didn't spare her a glance. He went right on speaking to David as if she weren't even there. "Just follow Skip and Nadine—" who were already heading out the door "—Suzette will go with you. She's very knowledgeable about music on the island. She'll be able to give you an overview. Afterward the two of you can talk more with Skip and Nadine if you want to."

"Great idea," Suzette said right on cue. "And I can help you find your way back to the Moonstone in the dark," she offered with a light laugh. "It's sometimes a little tricky."

David looked like he might have other ideas, but apparently years of being polite had taken their toll. He gave Fiona an apologetic smile, then turned to Suzette. "Thanks very much," he said. "That would be brilliant."

He bade farewell to everyone else, then turned to Fiona. "I'll see you tomorrow," he said, lingering as Lachlan herded them out of the restaurant and down the steps.

"I'll be around," Fiona assured him. "I'll be working at home in the morning and in Carin's shop in the afternoon."

"If you want her, I can spare her for an hour or two," Carin offered helpfully.

"I'm sure David won't need anywhere near that much of her time," Lachlan said briskly, coming back for them, holding the door and looking impatient. "He's a busy man. Go on now," he urged David and Suzette. "Must be almost time for the first set." Sounds of tuning and a bit of percussion were already coming from the Grouper. "You won't want to miss anything."

"Are you coming?" David asked Carin and Nathan politely.

Carin shook her head. "We'll be heading home," Carin

said. "Wouldn't do to leave Lacey on her own with Josh too long."

Nathan shuddered. "Heaven only knows what he will have got into." Josh was one—and a force to be reckoned with.

Fiona, who had baby-sat him herself a time or two, grinned. "He's just like Mike's boys were at that age." Over the years she'd baby-sat Tom and Peter a fair amount and had enjoyed it. She'd always intended to have children of her own. But that was back when she'd thought life was something she could plan.

And now?

Now she had Sparks. At least Sparks, even if he did say so himself, was a spectacular cat.

"I'll see you tomorrow," she said to Carin and Nathan. "You, too," she said to David. "It was lovely to meet you. Enjoy the steel band. Nice to see you again," she said to Suzette.

And then she turned to Lachlan who was looking decidedly irritable for no reason at all. "Thank you very much for dinner," she said in a proper, well-brought-up fashion. Her mother would have been proud. "It was kind of you to invite me."

Even though she knew now that he hadn't.

"It was, wasn't it?" he said smoothly. And to her amazement, instead of following David and Suzette or heading back to the Moonstone, he took her firmly by the arm and started down the hill with her.

She tried wriggling out of his grasp, but he only slid his hand down until his fingers laced with hers.

"What," she demanded through her teeth, "are you doing?"

"Walking you home."

"I don't need you to walk me home!"

"Too bad. I brought you. I'm taking you home."

"It's not necessary."

But apparently she wasn't convincing. Lachlan didn't answer He didn't let go of her hand either. His fingers were warm and rough against hers. Fiona felt a frisson of definite sexual awareness skitter up her spine.

"What was that business about me having to work?" she demanded.

He didn't answer that either.

"Lachlan?"

But he just strode on, and Fiona, if she didn't want to be dragged, had to practically run to keep up with him. Good thing she'd forgone Julie's dressy heels for her own sandals.

They went past Carin's old house, where Lachlan's sister, Molly, was now living. She was sitting on her front porch talking to Miss Saffron, the old lady who lived next door. Molly's eyes widened slightly at the sight of them together.

Miss Saffron waved gaily.

Fiona waved back and tried to look as if she wasn't being abducted, which was what it felt like. "What are you so mad about?"

"I'm not mad."

"You just naturally steam from the ears?"

He shot her a hard look. But not until they reached Fiona's porch did he ease his grip on her hand. She wiggled her fingers experimentally. They might get feeling in them again sometime next week.

"Well, that was nice," she said brightly because she certainly didn't know what else to say. "A lovely evening. A wonderful dinner. And now I've met an earl—"

"And flirted with him," Lachlan said harshly.

Fiona blinked as much at the tone as the words. She could hardly deny them. And why should she?

"I'm allowed," she said mildly. "And he didn't seem to mind. Actually," she reflected, "I think he quite enjoyed it. Now, I think I'll go in and get a good night's sleep since I have to be up early. Thank you for seeing me home," she added with a certain amount of irony.

But he didn't leave. He just stood there staring at her.

Fiona's brows lifted. "What? Do you want a tip?"

Even in the dim glow from the porch light, she saw a muscle in his temple twitch. "No, I do not want a tip. I want…this!"

And suddenly, astonishingly, he was kissing her.

His lips came down hard on hers, demanding, insistent, hungry. His arms wrapped around her, his chest pressed against hers.

It was what her brother Mike used to call a "full-body kiss." Very like the one Lachlan had given her when he'd taken her to his boat.

And just as she'd given in to it then, Fiona's resistance was no proof against it now. As perverse, annoying and irritating as it was, her determination melted, her defenses crumbled.

She was putty in his hands. Again. But unlike last time, there was no water to topple them into!

She moaned. Her lips parted under his, welcoming his urgency, inviting his invasion. All her childhood dreams were reawakened. All her longings surged within.

Fool, fool, fool! she called herself. But she wanted it— wanted him!

And then, all at once, Lachlan pulled back. His arms which had wrapped her let her go, and he stood breathing harshly, eyes glinting as he stared down into her eyes.

"Next time you want to flirt with someone, I'm available."

And then he spun on his heel, stalked down the steps and out the front gate without looking back.

CHAPTER FIVE

IT DIDN'T MAKE SENSE.

Fiona lay in her narrow bed, feeling Lachlan's kiss against her mouth, reliving it over and over, and wondering what on earth *that* was all about!

Next time you want to flirt with someone, I'm available.

He hadn't been jealous of David surely?

Of course not!

Lachlan McGillivray would never be jealous of anyone. Not even an earl. He'd have no reason. He could have any woman he wanted.

He could, she thought grimly, have had *her!*

He was the one who'd broken off the kiss.

So why—?

Was he simply being possessive? Pelican Cay was *his* island. Therefore, as an islander, Fiona belonged to him. Probably, she thought.

Jerk.

Oh yes. But God, what a kisser he was!

The first time she'd been kissed by Lachlan McGillivray, the night he'd taken her on to his boat, it had very nearly blown her mind.

Fiona had kissed men before—a few. Well, admittedly, very few. And she'd been kissed by them. So she wasn't a complete novice.

But she'd never had a kiss like that one. Had never even imagined such kisses existed. It had promised things that Fiona could only guess at.

But as much as she'd wanted it—and more—from

Lachlan McGillivray for years and years, the one thing she knew it didn't promise was forever. What Lachlan wanted—a night of sex—and what she wanted—a lasting love—weren't close to the same thing.

So to save them both making a huge mistake, she'd tipped them into the water.

Afterward she'd managed to convince herself that the effect of his kiss had been a fluke. The reason it had had such an effect was because she'd wanted it for so long— that was all.

But it wasn't all.

Dear God, no, it wasn't—because it had happened again tonight.

She'd nearly ignited from the fire his kiss had fanned between them. Her common sense and instinct for self-preservation had flat-out deserted her. God knew where it would have ended if Lachlan hadn't pulled back.

Well, actually Fiona was afraid she knew, too.

And how mortifying was that.

Especially since, up until the kiss, she thought she'd handled the evening very well. Her nerves had calmed under Julie's enthusiastic support. And her sister-in-law's dress had given her the confidence that she at least looked as if she belonged there.

The dinner had gone well. She'd chatted easily with David—thanks more to his charm than her social skills, no doubt. But still, thinking back over the evening, she felt good about it.

Everything had been perfect—until David had kissed her.

What? No. That wasn't right. David hadn't kissed her.

But he had, she remembered. They'd been discussing the possibility of her giving talks to his tour groups, and she'd hesitated, then agreed to at least consider it. And he'd been delighted and he'd kissed her.

A peck on the cheek, nothing more. Hardly even memorable. And the next second Lachlan was on his feet, asking for the check, and practically herding them out the door as he did so.

Surely one hadn't caused the other!

No, of course it hadn't. He'd simply looked at his watch, realized it was time for Skip and Nadine to be heading off for the Grouper. It made perfect sense.

Everything made sense.

Except why he'd been so irritated when he'd walked her home... And why he'd kissed her.

Was he embarrassed by her flirting with David?

It hadn't meant anything! A man like David Grantham— an *earl*, for heaven's sake!—was hardly going to be interested in a woman like her. Even so, it had been fun. Exhilarating. And entirely without the knife-edge of danger that flirting with Lachlan would have inspired.

Next time you want to flirt with someone, I'm available.

She didn't dare flirt with Lachlan, she thought, pressing her fingers once more against her mouth. Because with Lachlan it would mean something.

Even now she could taste his kiss, could feel the press of his lips against hers, could—

Stop it! She had to stop it!

She flipped over and pounded the pillow. It was nearly midnight. He would be here at five-thirty. She would have to look at his naked body again. She would have to begin to shape the terra-cotta, define the muscles, the hard planes and sharp angles she'd roughed in today. More things she didn't need to think about!

And yet she couldn't stop. It was so much more compelling than her cutout sculptures, more exciting than *The King of the Beach*.

Oh dear God. She sat up like a jack-in-the-box. *The King of the Beach!*

That was the work she had to do!

She scrambled out of bed and began pulling on her shorts and shirt. They'd made a deal, she and Lachlan. He'd pose nude and she'd remove her sculpture from in front of the Moonstone. Of course he'd said she didn't have to.

But they'd agreed. He'd done his part. He was going to do it again in a few short hours. And she needed to do hers. She wouldn't take it down entirely. She'd move it.

It was only fair. She had to keep her part of the bargain. It was a matter of honor.

WHY THE HELL HAD HE KISSED HER?

Lachlan prowled his room at the Moonstone, practically caroming off the walls, jamming his hands into his pockets, kicking at the rug underfoot, trying to find a logical answer to a totally illogical behavior.

And the answer was: because, damn it, he couldn't *not* kiss her!

He'd been dying to kiss her all day long—ever since he'd watched her in her studio that morning. He'd felt the same desire when he'd gone to the bakery in the afternoon to invite her to dinner.

And then, at dinner, watching her bat her eyelashes and flirt with David Bloody Grantham—letting Grantham *kiss* her!—it had been all Lachlan could do to keep his hands to himself.

He was a goalkeeper, damn it! He defended what was his—and Fiona Dunbar was his!

His!

He'd known her for years—ever since she was a pesky, bony, carrot-topped kid! And he was damned if he was going to watch her get her head turned by some jumped-up aristocrat!

She might think it was no big deal to flirt with a toff like David Grantham. But Lachlan knew better. Grantham would take advantage. She'd fall for him like a ton of bricks. Then he'd go back to England and she'd have a broken heart!

There was no way Lachlan was going to let that happen. No way at all.

He paced and paced some more. Cracked his knuckles. Raked his fingers through his hair. Finally the room wouldn't hold him any longer. He'd drive the couple crazy who were staying in the room below his.

He needed an outlet for his frustration. Something physical. And since punching Grantham's lights out wasn't a possibility (bad for business) he decided to take his frustration down to the beach.

He needed to do something hard, long and arduous. He didn't care as long as it took the edge off his irritation. What would really take the edge off, he knew, would be to go back to Fiona's and do more than kiss her!

But he couldn't. She wasn't ready for that.

Not yet.

But he'd felt her response tonight. He probably—no, *definitely*—could have had his way with her.

But he was damned if he'd be second best to Grantham. When Lachlan McGillivray took Fiona Dunbar to bed it would be because she wanted him—and only him.

The moon was up when he hit the beach, digging his toes into the still-warm sand. He considered running. But his body was hot and still hungry, so he crossed the soft sand into the water and dove beneath a wave. He struck out swimming along the beach just beyond the line of the surf. The temperature was warm even at nearly midnight in late June. But the water, though barely less than tepid, felt good on his burning skin.

He swam steadily, determinedly, making his body work, taking the edge off the fire that burned within. He swam to the point, then turned and plowed his way back again. Even so he'd barely taken the edge off by the time he reached the beach in front of the Moonstone and slogged ashore.

He stood dripping, heart pounding, as the incoming tide lapped his feet and he tipped his head back and drew in great lungfuls of air. Then, straightening again, he looked up toward the inn. There were a few lights still on behind curtained or shuttered windows. Silhouetted in front of them was Fiona's *The King of the Beach.*

What the hell?

Someone was climbing up Fiona's sculpture!

Indignant, annoyed, furious all over again—this time on her behalf—Lachlan sprinted up the beach toward the culprit.

"Hey!" he shouted. "What do you think you're— Oh, hell. Watch it!" he choked out as, at the sound of his furious voice, the figure jerked up, flailed for balance, then fell backward on to the sand.

Lachlan raced up to the still figure. "Are you—? *Fiona?*" He was somewhere between furious and indignant *at* her now.

The only sound that came in reply was a wheeze. Then she moved and gasped, "You...scared the...life...out of me!"

He crouched next to her, dripping water on her, demanding, "What the hell were you doing up there? Stay still," he commanded, patting her, trying to assess her injuries.

She gasped again and batted his hands away. "Stop that!"

But he didn't. He ran his hands over her ribs, her arms, her legs, dodging her slaps. "Where does it hurt?"

"It doesn't." She gave a little shake, then shoved her hair back from her face. "Well, it does actually—all over. But it was the fright more than anything else. For God's sake, Lachlan! What were you trying to do?" She struggled to sit up and slapped at him some more.

Moving out of range, Lachlan sat back on his heels. "It's dark. I didn't know it was you, did I? I thought someone was wrecking your sculpture."

"As if you'd care. You threatened to do it yourself." She'd managed to shove herself up so she leaned on her elbows.

"Take it easy," he insisted. "You might be bleeding internally."

"I'm *not* bleeding internally." She started to scramble to her feet.

So he got up with her, helping her, though she resisted, and managing to keep a hand on her once she got up which was how he could feel her trembling. "Why are you shaking?"

"Because you scared me!" She tried to brush him off. "I'm all right. Let go!"

He needed to keep a hand on her, though he couldn't have said why. He shook his head. "What the hell were you doing? It's after midnight!"

"I know what time it is. I didn't have time to get to it earlier."

"Get to what? Adding more? Trying to impress Lord Bloody Grantham?" He couldn't quite stop the sneer in his voice.

"I wasn't adding anything. I was taking it down," she said flatly. "As promised."

"I told you to leave it up. Grantham likes it."

"And you don't."

"Since when does what I like have anything to do with what you do? Other than encouraging you to do the opposite."

Her gaze flickered away. "That's not true. Anyway, we made a deal."

"And Grantham gave you a reprieve."

"We made our deal first. I'll move it."

He looked at her narrowly. "You must really want me naked."

It was too dark to see if she was blushing, but she didn't look him in the eye. "I want to finish my sculpture," she said tightly. "And I keep my word. I figured I'd take it down tonight and carry it over to the cricket grounds. I can put it up there."

"It would take you hours!"

Her jaw set. "I promised."

Stubborn woman. Lachlan studied her profile. "We'll see," he said at last. "We'll worry about whether or not you should take it down or not tomorrow." He took her hand and started to draw her up the beach toward the Moonstone, but she dug in her heels.

"What are you doing?"

"Come up and let's get a look at you. You could be hurt."

"I'm not hurt." She twisted out of his grasp and headed toward the path that led to town.

Lachlan went after her, started to take her arm, then decided he wouldn't gain anything by getting into a wrestling match with her. So he walked alongside her instead.

"What are you doing?" she demanded when he followed her right past the inn and on to the gravel road.

"Seeing you home."

"Don't be ridiculous."

"You're the one who's being ridiculous if you think I'm going to let you go by yourself when you've had a fall like that."

It wasn't just the possibility of her being hurt. There was the idiocy of her running around the island in the middle of the night. Anything could happen. He opened his mouth to say so, then closed it again. If he knew anything about Fiona Dunbar, it was that she would think she didn't need protecting.

Maybe she didn't.

But how the hell would he know unless he went with her?

"Go home," she said, eyes straight ahead, never slackening her pace. She turned off the road and on to the path that led through the mangroves. It was less gravel and more rock, ungraded, uneven and unlit.

Though well traveled during the day, it was not the way the Moonstone's guests came back from the village at night. They always took the road, which was only one lane but which had the occasional light and was far easier. It was also the long way around.

A sensible person would have taken it, Lachlan thought. So would a barefoot person—which he was. "The road—" he began.

"Is for tourists," Fiona said. "I know where I'm going."

She moved unerringly along the narrow path that wound through the mangroves over the dune and down the other side, winding its way toward the top of the village where it would meet the road again. Lachlan followed her. But he was the one who gritted his teeth as the rocks cut his feet. He was the one who tripped over a root and stumbled trying to keep up.

"Go back before you hurt yourself," she said, not turning.

"No."

An exasperated breath hissed between her teeth. "You're going to get cut to bits and I'm going to have to look after you!"

"Then you should have gone on the road."

She turned and glared at him.

He shrugged equably. "Your choice."

Apparently she got the point because she slowed her pace a little. She also said, "Watch out for those rocks," when there was a particularly rough bit and, "Mind the glass," where someone had broken a bottle.

"Thanks," he said.

She grunted.

As they came into town he could hear the band at the Grouper still going strong. There were a few people on the street, though none he knew, and Fiona didn't speak to anyone. They walked silently down the hill, along the quay and stopped when they reached Fiona's front gate.

"I suppose you expect me to invite you in," she said gruffly. "Put some antiseptic on those cuts."

He shrugged and told her the truth. "I'm coming in whether you invite me or not."

She opened her mouth, then gave him a sharp look, shrugged and turned to open the gate. "Suit yourself."

"See," he said when they got inside and he could examine her more closely. "You're all scraped up." She had a cut on her arm and a long abrasion on the outside of her right leg where she must have scraped herself on one of the driftwood spars as she fell.

Fiona looked at them dispassionately. "No big deal," she said. "You probably hurt your feet more."

"I'll live."

She looked at his bloody feet and shook her head. "You can wash them in the bathroom and put some antiseptic on. Coral cuts can get infected easily. There's some Band-Aids there, too. Come on." She led the way upstairs and while he washed his feet, she cleaned her arm and her leg.

"See," she said when they were done and back downstairs again. "It was totally silly for you to come with me. I'm fine. You're worse. You should call Maurice or one of the other taxis to drive you home."

"I'm not going home."

She stared at him. "Excuse me?"

"I'm not going home," he said. "I'm staying here."

"The hell you are! I don't recall inviting you to do anything of the sort."

"Perhaps because you're concussed," he said mildly.

"I am not concussed! I'm perfectly fine. I have a cut on my arm and a scraped leg. That's all."

"You could have internal injuries. You fell."

"I knocked the wind out of myself."

"That's what Joaquin thought," he said. "A friend of mine," he explained. "He fell off a motorcycle."

"Oh, well, a motorcycle. What do you expect?"

"He wasn't going fast, just slid the bike in some mud. He didn't think he was hurt, either," Lachlan went on. "Got up, got back on the bike, went home. And nearly died from a burst spleen."

"Lachlan, I don't have a burst spleen."

"You don't know that."

"Well, I'm not going to the doctor to find out."

"You could."

"Oh, yes. Sure." Fiona glanced at her watch. "At twenty past one in the morning? He'd appreciate that."

"It's his job. My dad would have been glad to see you."

"Your dad was a saint. Gerry—Doc Rasmussen—is just a doctor. A good one, but still—I'm not going to bother him. I'll be fine, Lachlan. Go home."

He shook his head. "No. I'll sleep on the couch."

"What?"

"Unless—" he suggested "—you want me to sleep with you."

She gaped at him. "You can't—I won't—!"

"Look, Fiona. Be sensible. It's almost one-thirty, as you just pointed out," he said. "It will take me until two to get home—"

"Not if you call Maurice."

"—and I have to be up before five to get back over here. No. Thanks. I need more sleep than that. Not that I would sleep anyway, worrying about you. No. I'm staying. That way I can check on you." He folded his arms and smiled amiably at her. "Or you could try to throw me out."

Fiona muttered under her breath. She scowled. She kicked at the rug underfoot. Finally she glared at him. "Fine," she said at last. "Stay. Go ahead. Try to sleep on it. It's lumpy. Very lumpy."

He barely spared it a glance. "It will do." He had undoubtedly slept on worse.

"But you're not 'checking' on me."

That's what you think. But he didn't say it. "Got a blanket?" he asked.

She made a huffing sound, then stalked back upstairs and came down moments later with a cotton blanket which she flung at him. "Sleep tight."

Then she turned and stomped back up the stairs.

Lachlan listened to her bang the door to her bedroom.

He heard sounds of her moving around, then all was quiet. He started to move to shut off the light when he heard a sudden slapping noise and Fiona's cat was sitting just inside the cat flap, eyeing him curiously.

"Don't mind me," he told the cat. "I'm just watching out for your pain in the neck mistress."

The cat didn't seem perturbed. He washed his paws, then yawned and found a comfortable chair to sleep in.

Lachlan stripped off his damp cutoffs and settled on the couch under the blanket. Fiona was right. The couch was lumpy. Very lumpy.

But he had no intention of leaving. He hadn't been joking about what had happened to Joaquin. It had been a freaky thing, but when you'd been there and seen it happen, you didn't forget. Please, God, it wouldn't happen to Fiona. But better safe than sorry.

He stretched and settled in, elbowing the most annoying of the lumps. It wasn't a bad place to be—in Fiona's living room. It wasn't her bedroom, but it was close.

A lot closer to her than Lord David Bloody Grantham was.

Lachlan felt as if he'd made a particularly spectacular save.

"Argh!" Fiona reached out and groped for her alarm clock, which was perversely tooting "Oh, What a Beautiful Morning."

It had been a joke gift from her brother Mike who knew how badly she hated to get up early. It wasn't so bad to have it doing its zip-a-dee-do-dah best at the crack of noon whenever she needed to make an afternoon appointment.

But it was dire to hear it warbling before first light.

How could anyone tell what kind of a morning it was, Fiona thought, gnashing her teeth and smacking it into silence, when the sun wasn't even up yet?

Her head was pounding. Her mouth tasted like the bottom of her brothers' boat. She ached all over. And she couldn't imagine why in God's name she had set the damn thing when she *never—*

Oh God!

Ohgod, ohgod, ohgod.

She didn't have to imagine. She remembered.

She sat up straight, groaned and fell back against the pillows.

It all came back now—the dinner at Beaches, the promise of work for David Grantham, the walk home with Lachlan.

The Kiss.

Dear God, yes, The Kiss.

And later—*after* The Kiss—when she'd been taking down *The King of the Beach,* Lachlan had appeared out of nowhere, shouting at her, startling her, making her lose her balance and fall.

That explained the aches. She'd got the wind knocked out of her. And Lachlan had come to crouch beside her and drip water all over her because he'd obviously been swimming, the idiot, all by himself which everyone knew you weren't supposed to do. And she'd scrambled to her feet, tried to brush him off, and Lachlan had refused to be brushed.

He'd walked her all the way home. Barefoot. He'd come in with her.

And, ye gods, he'd insisted on staying the night!

Yikes. He was likely—at this very moment—asleep downstairs on her very lumpy sofa.

That was the most horrible scenario she could come up with—until she heard a groan and the rustle of movement from the chair beside the bed.

"What the hell was that?" a gruff masculine voice growled.

Fiona sat bolt upright again, staring in horror. "*Lachlan?*"

"You were expecting Lord Bloody Grantham?"

Fiona scrabbled for her T-shirt and dragged it hastily

over her head. Why hadn't her father installed central air-conditioning years ago? Why had she ever thought it was a good idea to sleep in the buff?

She hauled the sheet over her. He hadn't seen—surely he hadn't!

"I wasn't expecting anyone!" she bit out, poking her head out from the T-shirt and reaching for her shorts. "You were downstairs."

He stood, yawned, stretched. The silhouette of a hard masculine frame was mouthwatering even in the semidarkness. "I was. Then I came up to see if you were dead yet."

"Oh, ha ha."

He shrugged and scrubbed a hand through his hair, then rubbed it over his face. "Been smarter if I'd kept an eye on Joaquin that night. I didn't and he damn near died. So I figured I ought to keep an eye on you."

"You were sleeping," Fiona reminded him.

"I dozed off. You weren't doing anything interesting."

And thank God for that, Fiona thought, mortified. She tried to untangle her feet from the sheet and poke them into her shorts.

"Don't bother on my account," Lachlan said, sounding amused. "I've already seen everything."

"You had no right!"

"Sorry," he said, not sounding sorry at all.

"You should be!"

"Did I lay a hand on you?"

"Well, no, but—"

"Then don't complain." He yawned again, so widely that she heard his jaw crack. Then he scratched his chest and ambled toward the bathroom.

"You're naked!"

"That makes two of us, then. See, I can count." White teeth flashed. "My shorts were wet, Fiona," he said patiently. "Sleeping in them didn't much appeal. Besides, it's nothing you haven't seen before."

"Yes, but—" But somehow it seemed a lot more personal in her bedroom!

"Fifteen minutes," Lachlan said, not waiting to hear her objection. "I'll meet you in the studio. Bring coffee."

SHE BROUGHT COFFEE.

Lachlan brought his watch—and wore it. It was the only thing he had on when he came into the studio twenty minutes later.

"I've got an eight o'clock meeting," he told her gruffly as he picked up one of the mugs and took a swallow. "I'm not missing this one."

"Of course not," Fiona said quickly. She was scurrying around businesslike and efficient, setting out her tools and uncovering the sculpture. "You're the one who said fifteen minutes," she reminded him. "I could have been ready in five."

Yeah, well, he couldn't have been. It had taken him time to get things under control. He was used to the early-morning behavior of his body. Awakening with an erection was no big deal. Happened all the time. Had nothing to do with lust. Ordinarily.

But then, ordinarily, he did not spend the night watching Fiona Dunbar sleep naked.

This morning lust had been a complicating issue.

It had taken an icy shower to resolve the problem. But even now it didn't feel settled. He felt twitchy, wired, edgy—walking the fine line of control.

Fiona was all business, just as she'd been yesterday. She focused on the sculpture, studying it from this angle and that, running her fingers over it, murmuring to herself. Then she nodded and scooped up some clay, slapped it on to the buttocks of her sculpture and set to work.

Lachlan stared off into space, did a few multiplication tables, tried to maintain his composure. But his mind kept drifting back to the woman across the room.

If she had been flustered by discovering he'd seen her naked, she'd got over it quick.

A whole lot quicker than he was getting over it, that was for damn sure.

He'd been absolutely serious when he'd told her he intended to check on her. Joaquin's injury had been too recent. It had been too nearly fatal. Of course such a thing wasn't likely to happen again. But blunt trauma was blunt trauma. And how likely had it been to happen in the first place?

So he'd stayed on the sofa, had got acquainted with each and every lump. And finally, after an hour, he'd got up and, wrapping the blanket around him, had quietly climbed the stairs and eased open the door to her room. He hadn't gone to spy on her. He'd simply wanted to check to be sure she was still breathing.

She was breathing, all right.

But one look at her lying nude on top of the sheets and he nearly wasn't!

He'd stood transfixed in the doorway, heart slamming against the wall of his chest, as he'd stared at her asleep in the moonlit room.

All the rampaging lust he'd attempted to work off during his midnight swim came flooding back. His mouth went dry, his palms got damp, and his whole body grew taut at the sight of her.

She'd been sound asleep. Resting easily. Comfortably. He could see the rise and fall of her moon-washed breasts. He couldn't look away.

In fact, he'd moved closer. He had slipped right into the room and had gone to stand by the side of the bed. There he'd stood looking down on her, clenching his fists against the longing to lie down next to her and touch her, to stroke her smooth skin, to cup her breasts in his palms, to kiss the line of her jaw and run his hands down her thighs to part—

Oh hell, he couldn't go there! Not now!

Quick! Penguins! Icebergs!

The sinking of the bloody *Titanic!*

But it didn't do a damn bit of good.

He bolted off the modeling stand, spilling his coffee as he headed for the bathroom. "Gotta leave!" he muttered, leaving Fiona to look up from the sculpture and stare after him, openmouthed in his wake.

"But—" Footsteps came pattering after him.

He banged shut the bathroom door.

"Lachlan? Is something wrong?"

Body quivering, he panted. "Nothing's wrong!"

"Then why—?"

Oh hell, oh hell, oh hell.

"Lachlan?"

"I've got an appointment I just remembered!"

"At six-thirty in the morning?"

"Yes." He dragged on his damp cold shorts and hoped they would do the job that the iceberg and the *Titanic* hadn't. It took a while. He waited to hear the footsteps moving away.

As soon as he was presentable, he rubbed a hand over his face, sucked in a deep breath and opened the door.

Fiona was standing in the doorway to her studio, looking at him irritably. "What's going on?"

"Sorry. Just…remembered something I had to do."

Her gaze narrowed. "I was just getting started, Lachlan."

He grimaced wryly as he hurried past her down the stairs. "Yeah. Me, too."

SHE HAD MISSED SOMETHING. Fiona was sure of it.

Lachlan had been there, standing perfectly still one minute—and gone the next.

She banged around the studio after he left, trying to make sense of his vanishing act, trying to work on the sculpture without him, getting nowhere.

Was it something she had done? Something she had said?

But she had done nothing except begin to work. And she'd said absolutely nothing at all.

If she didn't know better, she would think he had panicked.

But that was ridiculous.

She was the one who had reason to panic! She was the one who'd awakened and discovered he'd spent the night within touching distance of her naked body!

And been so inspired that he'd fallen asleep! Whatever passion last night's kiss had stirred in him, the sight of her in the nude had obviously given him definite second thoughts. Unfortunately it still had the power to heat her blood.

And the sight of a nude Lachlan McGillivray was driving her nuts.

She'd managed to sublimate her avid interest yesterday by channeling it into the clay, by trying to capture his planes and angles, muscles and bones. On an artistic level she'd begun to succeed.

But far from encouraging her indifference, it had made her want Lachlan McGillivray more than she ever had before.

"Bah!" She tossed a damp towel over the sculpture of his nakedness and tried to focus on this week's cutouts for Carin. But she couldn't get lost in her work the way she usually did.

And when the phone rang, she was grateful for the diversion. "Hello?"

"Is it true?" Julie asked without preamble. "Are you and Lachlan McGillivray having an affair?"

CHAPTER SIX

"WHAT?"

Fiona sat down with a thump. Lucky for Sparks he'd just vacated the chair she landed in.

"Trina said she saw him coming out of your place when she got off work this morning," Julie reported. "And Miss Saffron said she saw him hightailing up the hill at the crack of dawn."

Oh God.

At Fiona's total stunned silence, Julie went on quickly, "Of course it's really none of anybody's business, but—"

No, it wasn't. But this was Pelican Cay and one person's business was always everyone else's business. Trina was the weather girl on the local radio station. Miss Saffron was the source of much of what passed for island "news." Between the two of them—

"No!" Fiona blurted before it went any further. "Lachlan and I are *not* having an affair."

"Oh." Julie sounded almost disappointed.

"Julie!"

"I mean, of course you're not," her sister-in-law said hastily. "That's what I told them…" she added, her voice trailing off inconclusively.

But…

Fiona could hear the word even though it wasn't there.

"You're an adult, after all," Julie said after a moment. "And they did see him. So if you were…"

"Lachlan McGillivray and I are not having an affair!"

Julie went silent on the other end of the line.

"Look," Fiona said desperately, knowing she couldn't tell Julie why Lachlan had really been here. He'd have her head if she did that. But she clearly wasn't going to be able to pretend both Miss Saffron *and* Trina had been seeing things. "Yes, Lachlan was here this morning, but it was no big deal."

"No big deal," her sister-in-law echoed in the tone she might have used if Ahab had said Moby Dick was not a very big whale.

"There's a simple explanation," Fiona insisted. "Last night, after I got home from the dinner at Beaches—the dress was great, by the way—I went to bed. By myself," she added firmly before Julie could ask. "And I suddenly realized, about midnight, that I'd promised to move *The King of the Beach*."

"Move the—?" Julie sputtered. "Why? Where?"

"I thought I'd take him over by the cricket ground," Fiona said, deliberately answering the second question and not the first. "So I went down to get started."

"At midnight?"

"I couldn't sleep. I was too excited. David—Lord Grantham—really liked my work. He thought the King was super, but he liked the rest of it, too. He thinks I have talent—"

"Of course you have talent!" Julie said staunchly.

"And he wants to feature me. He wants me to give talks to the groups that come on tours."

"Talks? To the tourists? Oh, Fee! That's marvelous! No wonder you couldn't sleep!" Julie, as Fiona had known she would, completely bought this as a reason for lying awake. There was no need to explain about The Kiss at all.

"He wants to use a photo of it for his tour brochure," she went on. "So I thought I'd better get it moved quick."

"But why move it at all?"

"Because I told Lachlan I would. It does sort of interfere with the serene upscale ambience of the Moonstone."

"I thought that was the whole point," Julie said drily.

"Yes, well, I think I made my point. And I sort of, um, owe Lachlan one." Not that she was going to say what for, of course. "Anyway, I was taking it down, and I was right up at the top, taking off the head—that big bucket, you know? And all of a sudden I heard this voice yell at me, and I lost my balance and fell."

"Oh my God! Are you—?"

"I'm fine," Fiona said firmly. "I just got the wind knocked out of me."

"Thank heavens. Who yelled? Those rackety boys go down to the beach at night, I know. If they—"

"Lachlan yelled. He thought I was a vandal wrecking the sculpture."

"I'd have thought he would have paid any vandal who did that," Julie said.

"That's what I said. But he's changed his tune a little. He wants to keep Grantham happy. Anyway, he was worried about my having fallen, so he walked home with me."

"And spent the night?" Julie said doubtfully.

"Actually, yes. He said a friend of his had almost died of a blunt trauma injury. He was worried I would. He wanted me to go to the doctor, and I wouldn't. Can you imagine me getting Gerry up in the middle of the night and saying I'd fallen off my sculpture?"

"Not really." Julie knew Gerry Rasmussen as well as Fiona did.

"Exactly. So he stayed."

"All night?" Julie repeated. Obviously this was the difficult part to get past.

"On the couch."

"Lachlan McGillivray spent all night on your lumpy couch?" Julie said after a long moment. She still sounded doubtful, but at least she wasn't saying, *Oh, go on! That's the biggest laugh I've had in months.*

"Yes."

"To make sure you didn't die?"

"Exactly."

There was another very long assessing pause on the other end of the line.

"I see," Julie said at last. "Well, that explains it. I understand perfectly why he was leaving your place this morning. Makes complete sense."

Fiona smiled. "Good."

"I'll be sure to tell Trina and Miss Saffron and anyone else who asks."

"Thank you." Disaster averted, Fiona heaved a huge sigh of relief.

Long pause.

"So why did they see him leaving *yesterday* morning as well?" Julie asked.

THE THING ABOUT LIVING on an island, which Lachlan had forgotten somewhere along the way, was that wherever you went, there you were—and so was the person you were trying to avoid.

Not that he was trying to *avoid* Fiona Dunbar exactly.

It was just that he needed some space. He needed to think!

And he couldn't seem to do it when he was around her. Fiona had a way of getting under his skin, pushing his buttons, making him nuts without even realizing it.

Or maybe she did.

Maybe this King-of-the-Beach-building, naked-male-terra-cotta-sculpting, sleeping-in-the-nude business was all a concerted effort to make him so crazy with unbridled, unsatisfied desire that he would say the hell with it, throw in the towel, sell the inn, leave the island and head to the other ends of the earth, putting as much of it between himself and Fiona Dunbar as he possibly could!

In the heat of the moment, he could believe that. And just recently he was having a lot of very heated moments.

So he did what any sane man would do when he looked out his window that afternoon and saw that the object of every one of his thoughts since he'd left her house that morning was shinnying up what was left of a ten-foot-high sculpture, her long tanned bare legs wrapped intimately around its midsection.

He bolted.

"Dooley needs me at the Sandpiper," he told Suzette as he headed out the door. "I'll be gone a few days. A week. I don't know!"

Suzette looked up from her computer and frowned. "Dooley called? I thought you had that sorted."

"Nope. Not yet. Emergency," Lachlan said. Well, how else would you describe it? If he shut his eyes all he could see was Fiona's bare midriff and her honey-tan legs.

"But—"

"Gotta go. Call Hugh and tell him I need him to fly me over. Now!"

Suzette blinked, then picked up the phone. But as she did she studied him. "You look a little flushed, Lachlan. Are you all right?"

THERE HAD TO BE a handful of people on Pelican Cay—other than children and tourists—who did not believe Fiona and Lachlan were having an affair.

Had to be, Fiona assured herself. But damned if she knew who they were.

Not that anyone was being judgmental about it.

On the contrary, Tony, her boss at the bakery, started to ask if she would work the morning shift on the weekend, then stopped himself abruptly, grinned and said, "Never mind. You'll be needing your sleep now more than ever, won't you?"

"I will?" Fiona said, determinedly guileless. "Why?"

It was almost gratifying to watch Tony's face turn red. It would have been more gratifying if he'd backtracked and admitted he might be mistaken. He didn't.

Neither did Nikki, the other waitress, who said, "Lucky you. I think he's really hot."

Fiona didn't have to ask who she meant. And what was

she supposed to say? *I wouldn't know.* Well, actually she tried saying that.

But Nikki just giggled and said, "I'd be discreet, too."

Even Carin seemed to think she and Lachlan were actually having an affair. She didn't say anything directly when Fiona stopped into the shop, because Carin was the most discreet person Fiona knew. But she gave Fiona a knowing look above the heads of a couple of customers.

And before Fiona left, Carin gave her shoulders a squeeze and said, "Good for you."

Short of taking out an ad in the local weekly paper denying that she and Lachlan were sleeping together, Fiona didn't know what to do.

Besides, even if she had, who would believe her?

Because, as her other sister-in-law, Claire, said cheerfully that evening, when she stopped by on her way home from visiting Miss Saffron, "It's not like we all wouldn't like to sleep with Lachlan McGillivray!"

"I'm not—" Fiona began.

But Claire just shook her head. She sat in the rocker in the living room, scratching Sparks under the chin and smiling. "I'm just so happy for you," she said. "We're all happy for you, Fee. Well, actually Mike has threatened to punch his lights out if he hurts you, but we're really glad you've found someone. We were getting worried..."

"Worried?"

Claire shrugged. "You know, after Dad died, you seemed so lost and alone. You gave him so much time, so much of yourself, your life...and then he was gone." She sighed. "And, let's face it, Mike and Paul still feel guilty."

"Guilty? Why on earth?" Fiona had never heard this before. She stared at her sister-in-law in amazement.

Claire, encouraged and warming to a topic that had apparently been discussed by the entire family—sans Fiona—went on firmly. "They thought they should have done more for Dad. For you. To take the burden off you. They were afraid that you weren't ever going to have a life and they should have been more aware all along.''

"That's nonsense.''

"That's the way they felt. And then Dad died and they thought, now she'll do something. And you didn't.''

"I did!''

"Not really,'' Claire said frankly. "You kept doing what you had been doing. And I have to admit, I got a little worried too when months went by and you didn't go anywhere or do anything.''

"I was working,'' Fiona defended herself. "I didn't go into a shell, you know. I just went on. I didn't know I was supposed to just jump up and run out and change everything.''

"Of course you weren't. It was just them feeling guilty about the past. And hoping you'd do something—find someone—so they wouldn't feel that way. Julie and I both said you would, but it would take time.'' She looked at Fiona and suddenly beamed. "But now you have.''

Er.

"Well, I—''

"And thank God for that,'' Claire said fervently. "And what a man. Lachlan McGillivray. We'll have to buy you some red panties!'' she giggled.

"You will not!''

"Of course, Mike and Paul won't be happy until he's put a ring on your finger, but—''

"Claire, stop it! Don't let's rush things,'' Fiona said hastily.

"No, of course not.'' Claire sobered at once. "And I wouldn't rush things either, if I were you. But you're out of your rut now. Living again.'' She set Sparks on the floor and got up to give her sister-in-law a hug. "We're so glad, Fee. Just enjoy.''

ENJOY?

How on earth did you enjoy an affair you weren't having? Fiona prowled the house after Claire left.

"What am I going to do?" she asked Sparks.

Sparks had one answer to every question: feed me. He butted his head against her calves and wove between her ankles. He looked hopefully at his food dish for signs of filling, then at Fiona reproachfully when it did not.

"Oh, dear," she said finally, realizing she'd been prowling so much she'd missed his dinnertime. "Sorry." She fetched the fish scraps that Claire had brought for him and put them in his bowl.

All right with his world now, Sparks fell to eating.

If only a couple of fish heads would sort hers out, Fiona thought wearily. An affair with Lachlan? It would be laughable if it weren't so painfully tempting.

She needed to call Lachlan and tell him not to come in the morning. A third sighting and the island telegraph would have them on their way to the altar!

But she didn't have his mobile number and calling the inn would mean talking to Josie at the front desk. As soon as Josie spread the word that Fiona was calling Lachlan, things would go from bad to worse.

But no worse than him showing up here again tomorrow for the third day in a row.

What a mess.

The phone rang as she was pacing the floor trying to decide whether to call Lachlan or not. She snatched it up. "Hello?"

"Hey." The rough baritone was unmistakable.

She took a quick steadying breath. "Lachlan," she said and braced herself for his fury.

"I can't come in the morning," he said.

It was so *not* what she expected him to say that she didn't think she'd heard him right. "I— What?"

"I can't come," he repeated. "I'm at the Sandpiper. In the Abacos. Hugh flew me up this afternoon. My contractor quit and I've got half a dozen things need sorting out. Place is going to hell in a handbasket. Don't know how long I'll be away.''

"Oh," she said numbly. Then, "Oh!" as a great surge of relief hit her.

"So I hope it won't cause you too many problems.''

"No, no! It's fine," she said cheerfully. "No problem at all.''

"No?'' He sounded surprised.

"Absolutely not," she assured him. "I was thinking of giving you a call and telling you I could manage on my own for a while.'' *Yes!* she thought, dancing a happy little twirl around Sparks who looked askance at her. *Yes! Yes! Yes!*

"Is that right?'' Lachlan said slowly.

"Yes, of course. I didn't expect you to come every day.''

"Could've fooled me," she thought he said.

"What?''

"Nothing. Never mind. Well, fine. I'll, er, just see you when I get back, then.''

"Right. Fine. Don't hurry on my account.''

"I wouldn't think of it," Lachlan said drily.

AND WHAT, HE'D LIKE to know, was *that* all about?

Lachlan dropped the phone on the bed, jammed his hands into his back pockets and scowled out the window of the Sandpiper into the darkness.

He'd been prepared for Fiona to pitch a fit, to tell him he was a chicken, to make her ghastly gobbling sounds when he'd said he wasn't going to show up in the morning. He'd looked forward to arguing with her.

And she hadn't minded at all.

Minded, hell? She'd sounded pleased!

He scuffed at the bare boards underfoot, annoyed, and worse, annoyed that he was annoyed, when he knew he should be pleased.

He didn't *want* to pose nude, did he?

No, he definitely didn't want to do that.

If he was going to be naked and there was a woman in the room—particularly if she was Fiona Dunbar—then he wanted her to be naked, too.

He'd spent a lot of time recently thinking about being naked with Fiona Dunbar. Even here and now, fourteen hours after that early-morning fiasco, his body could still grow taut with desire at the thought of the two of them naked together.

"So stop thinking about it," he told himself.

It was, after all, what he'd intended to do by coming here. Out of sight, out of mind and all that.

But before he could forget her, he'd had to call and tell her he wasn't going to show up in the morning. He didn't want her thinking he'd stood her up for no reason.

He had a good reason. He was a responsible businessman with responsibilities and obligations and, apparently, a sense of prescience—because when he'd arrived at the Sandpiper this afternoon it was to have Sybil, his go-to girl come running up to tell him that Dooley the contractor had just quit.

The "emergency" he'd manufactured for Suzette's benefit had come to pass. And he had a ton of things to do as a result—dealings with electricians and plumbers and a temperamental woodworker, not to mention the roof that had caused Dooley to throw up his hands and quit—which would make it easy to forget Fiona Dunbar. And he fully intended to take his time doing them.

He'd get the Sandpiper on track again and head back to Pelican Cay only when he was damned good and ready.

But he wanted to know why the hell she was glad he wasn't coming tomorrow morning first!

IT DIDN'T MATTER that Lachlan wasn't here, Fiona thought. It didn't slow things down at all. At least that was what she tried telling herself in the morning when she worked on the terra-cotta sculpture.

But it wasn't the same working by herself. She didn't have that immediate point of reference for one thing. She couldn't simply look up and study what she was working on.

Besides that, there was a sense of vitality that was missing when her model wasn't here. There was always an energy wherever Lachlan was. Even when he wasn't moving, you could sense it, you could feel it.

She tried to capture it in her work, tried to imbue the clay with the tension that emanated from the man. Her hands shaped and formed, molded and stroked.

Made her want. Made her ache.

She'd hoped the experience would be therapeutic or at the very least a learning experience.

She supposed it was. She learned that she wasn't going to get Lachlan out of her system that easily.

Finally she gave up and went to work at the bakery. Tony winked at her and gave her a commiserating grin. "He'll be back soon."

There was no use pretending she didn't know who he was talking about.

"Next time maybe he'll take you with him," Tony suggested.

Which was the same thing Miss Saffron said when Fiona was passing her house on her way from the bakery to Carin's. And the same thing Elaine, who was working at Carin's that afternoon, said when Fiona stopped in there.

She finally took refuge from all this commiseration by going to the cricket field, where she set up the driftwood spars, anchored them securely, then climbed to the top of *The King of the Beach.* No one was going to offer solace to her up there.

But even there she couldn't get away from him—because while she worked she looked out over the cricket field which was usually no more than the pasture for a couple of local goats and horses. But this summer it had become a soccer pitch.

For the past two months it had been mowed and tended by a group of island boys. Goals had been put up at either end, and the island kids played soccer games and practiced soccer drills diligently and determinedly every afternoon because their coach told them to.

Their coach—Lachlan.

"He's a great coach," her nephew Tom, Mike's oldest boy, had said just last week. His eyes had shone as he'd told Fiona about the goal he'd scored when they'd played the kids from Coral Harbour.

"You should come watch sometime," his younger brother Peter urged, because while most of the island turned out for the kids' soccer games these days Fiona never had.

"Since they owe it all to you," her brother Mike had added with a grin when the boys had run back to play.

"Nonsense." Fiona had denied it vehemently.

"You wrote the letter to the editor," Paul reminded her. "What was it you said about giving back to the community?"

"I didn't mean just Lachlan," Fiona muttered, though that had certainly been, she recalled now, the implication.

"Shamed him into it." Julie had grinned. But last night she had speculated that perhaps Lachlan had taken on coaching the kids' soccer team for an entirely different reason. "I'll bet he did it because he was already sweet on you."

"He was not!" Fiona had really blushed then. "He wasn't," she insisted. "Isn't."

For all the good it had done.

But watching now, she knew that why ever he had done it, it had been good for the island children. They didn't just kick the ball around listlessly the way Fiona remembered.

These days they had purpose. They had drills, focus, energy, commitment. They knew what they were doing. And even without Lachlan there to supervise, they kept going.

"Most impressive," a cheerful masculine voice said from below.

Fiona jerked and looked down to see David Grantham squinting up at her.

"Yes, they're great. Lachlan's taught them a lot."

He glanced at the game going on in front of them, then back at Fiona. "So I hear. But I didn't mean the kids. I meant this." He patted the largest driftwood spar. "And you." His eyes traced the line of her long bare legs before meeting her eyes again. He grinned appreciatively.

Fiona felt suddenly self-conscious. "I'm trying to get him right," she said quickly. "Maybe you could make some suggestions?"

"I suggest you have dinner with me this evening."

It was on the tip of her tongue to say no. She was so used to saying no. But why not?

She no longer had to be home all the time. No one was waiting for her but Sparks. It would cause the Lachlan rumor to die a quicker death if she was seen out dining with someone else. She smiled. "I'd like that. Thank you."

He walked her home when she'd finished working on the King so he could learn where she lived. He admired her home, talking easily and knowledgeably about indigenous island architecture.

"Something else we might want to study on our tour," he said. "We can discuss it tonight. Shall I pick you up at seven-thirty?"

"Fine." Fiona smiled.

"We aren't only going to talk shop," David promised.

"But—" Fiona began quickly.

He cut her off with a smile. "Don't panic. We're just going to get to know each other. Okay?"

Fiona took a deep and, she hoped, steadying breath. "Yes," she said. "I'd like that."

SHE WASN'T HOME.

He'd been calling her all evening and she bloody wasn't home!

Where the hell was she? And what if it were an emergency, for crying out loud? Why didn't she have a mobile phone?

Lachlan punched in Fiona's number for the hundredth time that evening, scowling as he listened to it ring and ring and ring.

Damned woman didn't even have an answering machine!

"Hello?" Her answer—at last—startled him. So did the breathless tone.

"What's wrong?" he barked.

"Wrong?" He heard her gulp. "Not a thing. Why? What's wrong with you? Why are you calling?"

Why *was* he calling?

Hours ago he'd had a reason. He'd intended to tell her he was still working, that he wouldn't be there in the morning. Nothing important really, but he'd intended to be polite. Conscientious. That was then.

"Where were you?" he demanded now, not answering her question.

"Out to dinner," she said. "Is something wrong, Lachlan?"

He ploughed his fingers through his hair. "No. Yes. I— with who?"

"David," she said brightly. "Lord Grantham." As if he didn't bloody know! "We went to the Sand Dollar."

"The Sand Dollar?" It had taken the name from the old inn that had once been the Moonstone. In its new incarnation it was a flashy joint that appealed to the young tourists. Hardly the place for a low-key island girl. Lachlan gritted his teeth. "Is he there now?"

"At the Sand Dollar?"

God give him patience. "With you?"

"No. Did you want to talk to him? He just left. I showed him some of my other work."

Oh Christ! "You didn't!"

"What?" Then she seemed to realize what he meant. "No. Of course not. He wouldn't have known it was you anyway, would he?"

Lachlan didn't know. He didn't care. He breathed a very small sigh of relief. Not much relief. He didn't feel much relief. He felt—he didn't know what he felt. Annoyed. Irritated.

He'd worked his ass off all day, trying to do all the things that Dooley would have been doing, and at the same time trying to find someone to replace Dooley to oversee the operation while he was gone. Likely candidates weren't thick on the ground. And he'd been doing his best to be conscientious, to call and say he didn't know when he would be back.

Why bother? Obviously she didn't give a damn!

"Going to sculpt him next?" he snarled.

"What? Sculpt David? Oh, no. I don't think so." She gave a light laugh.

Because David Lord Bloody Grantham probably wasn't as big a sap as he was, Lachlan thought sourly. He cracked his knuckles and scowled out into the darkness.

"But we did talk about what I'm going to do next," Fiona went on.

"Oh? And what's that? More naked men? More trash?"

Fiona ignored his sniping as if he were a bad-tempered child. "David thinks if I'm serious about becoming a sculptor I ought to go away to school."

"*Go away?* Go away *where?* What the hell does Grantham know about it?"

"I don't know where yet for sure. It's just that there's no one I can study with on the island. When Carin was learning to paint, she had a mentor at least. But there isn't anyone on the island who can do that for me."

"So find one and bring one in."

"Oh, sure. Right. Get real, Lachlan."

"Well, why do you have to have someone?"

"It helps if I want to learn more. You went to university. You played soccer for coaches. You had mentors. There's just so much a person can do on their own. You reach a

certain level and you stop. I was going to go once,'' she
confided.

That surprised him because he thought she'd given up
the idea when she'd said earlier that she couldn't afford it.
"You were? When?"

"Before my dad got sick. I know, that was eons ago.
But I had applied. I was saving my money. I don't know
if I'd ever have got accepted, but I was going to try."

He heard a wistfulness in her voice he didn't think he'd
ever heard before. It made him uncomfortable.

"I was thinking I was too old to give it a shot now. But
David says why not? He says he knows a school in
England. He's going to get them to send me some infor-
mation."

David says...David says...

"Bully for him," Lachlan muttered under his breath.
"Well, that's interesting," he said gruffly. "And I guess
that's something to think about. Long way from home,
though. You might get homesick."

There was a pause. Then, "I might," Fiona allowed.
There was an even longer pause during which he hoped to
hell she was thinking about that—about missing the island,
missing her family, her friends.

Missing him.

Then she said, "Why did you call?"

"To be polite. I'm still working at the Sandpiper," he
told her brusquely. "I didn't want you expecting me tomorrow either."

"Not a problem," Fiona said. "Like I said yesterday,
absolutely no hurry."

"Yeah, well—" Lachlan wasn't so sure about that.

DAVID WAS AS GOOD as his word. He came by the next
evening and brought her information about the art school
in England he had mentioned.

"Actually there are three schools you might want to apply to," he told her as she poured them each a glass of

iced tea, then motioned him to go back out into the shade of the front porch. The overhead fan picked up what there was of a breeze and made sitting on the porch the best place to be.

Besides, the more people who saw her with a man other than Lachlan the better, Fiona thought. Last night's dinner had given a few people pause for thought if the looks they'd given her were anything to go by.

"I e-mailed my secretary and she contacted the admissions people at all of them," David was saying as he spread out some sheets on the wicker table. "Look here. I printed out their requirements. Sit down and I'll show you."

Obediently Fiona sat on the glider and David sat next to her. Their knees brushed. She moved hers away slightly.

David smiled at her. "There aren't too many hoops to jump through. They want letters of recommendation, primarily. I'll write you one, of course. Being a featured artist on a Grantham tour can't hurt."

"Certainly can't. That would be nice."

"And I'm sure Carin will write one for you. Nathan, too. I can show your work to a sculptor friend of mine in Edinburgh. He's a good judge. I'm sure he'd give you a good recommendation. And you can send those in along with your portfolio."

Her portfolio.

Of course she would have to send in a portfolio. As she'd told Lachlan, an artist had to have a portfolio. And what would she include in hers?

The seashell miniatures? The metal cut-outs? The sand castles all the tourists loved? *The King of the Beach?*

"Well, I—"

"It's late, of course, to be accepted for the autumn term. But sometimes there are openings due to cancellation. You can fill out the applications tonight. I'll take digital pictures of the sculptures and drawings you want to submit. Then you can send them out in the morning. The sooner we get you to England the better."

He was smiling at her. And there was something in the way he looked at her that said that "the sooner" and "the better" she got to England had nothing to do with her studying to be a sculptor.

Fiona flushed and took refuge behind her glass of tea. "I'd like to see England," she said as neutrally as she could. "And Scotland," she added. "My dad was from Scotland. He taught me to play the bagpipes."

"Bagpipes?" David looked perplexed.

"I don't play much anymore," Fiona told him. Only every once in a while, like this past spring when she'd still had hopes of driving out Lachlan.

"Well, I can show you Scotland, too," David said cheerfully. He reached out and brushed a strand of hair away from her face, then put his hand on her knee.

Suddenly the front gate crashed open and a harsh male voice drawled, "Well, isn't that sweet?"

"Lachlan!" Fiona jumped up, knocking David's hand away, spilling her tea everywhere.

Lachlan gave David a hard look and her a mocking smile. "Just thought you'd like to know I'm back."

CHAPTER SEVEN

SHE COULD HAVE LOOKED happier to see him.

He'd practically busted his butt to hire a replacement for Dooley, clue the man in on things and get back to Pelican Cay.

It hadn't been easy, and in the end he'd even had to bribe his damn brother to come and get him. Hugh had had "other things" to do that afternoon.

"What other things?" Lachlan had demanded.

"I met this redhead last night..." Hugh began lazily.

The last thing Lachlan wanted to talk about was redheads.

"Forget her! Just get the hell over here," he told his brother, "and I'll make your next helicopter payment."

At least Hugh had his priorities straight. He had arrived two hours later.

"So what's the rush?" Hugh said when Lachlan had flung his overnight bag into the plane and scrambled in after. "Fiona missing you?"

"*What?*" Lachlan stared at his brother, openmouthed in astonishment.

Hugh gave him a narrow look. "I said," he repeated slowly, "is Fiona missing you?"

Not at all sure where the conversation was going, Lachlan answered a question with a question. "What if she is?"

"I told you not to mess with her."

"I'm *not* messing with her!"

"Yeah, right." Hugh scrubbed a hand through his hair.

"Well, as long as she's happy. She has a right to be happy, damn it," he muttered almost to himself. Then he turned and leveled a hard look at Lachlan. "All I've got to say, bro, is you hurt her and you'll have me to answer to—*and* Mike *and* Paul *and* half the damn island."

"Why me?" Since when had Fiona Dunbar's happiness become his responsibility?

"Because you're the one having the affair with her!"

Oh yeah?

Not that he'd said so to Hugh, of course. He'd stone-walled Hugh totally. All that goalkeeping experience—where a guy didn't give anything away ever—had stood him in good stead.

Besides, far be it from him to protest that he wasn't sleeping with Fiona. It wouldn't be gallant. Especially not if she was the one who had said he was!

Had she said he was?

As soon as they'd landed, he'd headed straight over to Fiona's place to find out. His mind had been brimming with half a dozen fantasies on the way, all of them involving him stripping off his—*and her*—clothes the minute he got in the door.

He hadn't counted on finding Lord Bloody Grantham with his hand on Fiona's knee the minute he opened the gate!

Or Fiona scrabbling around mopping up iced tea and looking panic-stricken at the sight of him. So much for fantasies.

"Ah, McGillivray! Welcome back!" Trust Grantham to stand up and offer a gentlemanly handshake as if the two of them were at some blinking garden party. "Wondered where you'd got off to."

Lachlan gave Grantham's hand one quick shake and dropped it. "Some of us have work to do. I can see you've been busy." He turned the sarcasm on Fiona.

She blinked, puzzled, then managed a quick dazed smile. "Oh, you saw *The King of the Beach?* Yes, he's back up and overlooking the cricket field. I even added some new bits today. What did you think of the inner tube?''

Lachlan, who hadn't seen the inner tube and hadn't been talking about *The King of the Beach* at all, scowled. ''That's not what I meant.''

''Oh?'' She looked momentarily blank again, then said brightly, ''You mean the school applications?'' She picked up the papers that she'd dropped when she'd spilled the tea, waving them cheerfully. ''I'm just getting on them. David brought these over for me to fill out. Isn't that lovely? He's found three schools in England he thinks I should apply to.''

''Has he?'' Lachlan said through his teeth.

''Indeed,'' David agreed cheerfully. ''Two in the south and one up north. I was just about to offer to help her fill them out and get her portfolio together...'' He smiled and let the sentence dangle unfinished, waiting expectantly for Lachlan to do the polite thing and leave.

Lachlan looked at Fiona. She wasn't inviting him to stay, either.

''Fine,'' he said through his teeth because he was damned if he was going to beg to be invited to stick around. ''You do that. I'll be back,'' he promised her. ''At the regular time.''

Grantham's brows shot up.

''See you then,'' Lachlan said flatly. It wasn't a question. They both knew it.

IT WAS JUST AS WELL David stayed until nearly midnight helping her get together her portfolio. It kept her occupied, kept her focused, kept her from thinking about Lachlan every second.

As it was she thought about him every other second.

What was she going to say to him in the morning?

Should she say something *before* morning? Should she call him and tell him the rumor that was going around? Tell him he should stay away or he'd be feeding it.

But she couldn't call him right away because David had been there. And after David left it was too late.

All she could do then was pace the floor or go to bed and toss and turn. She did first one and then the other. Neither helped. Neither banished him from her mind.

Nothing banished him from her mind because, heaven help her, she was in love with him.

The tossing and turning stopped abruptly and Fiona lay very still and stared at the ceiling and made herself say the words out loud. "I'm in love with him."

And how foolish and stupid and senseless was that?

Very. But it was also very true.

The truth of it had hit her right in the gut when the gate had opened tonight and Lachlan had strode into the yard and announced he was back.

Until that moment she'd told herself what mattered was moving on, developing her talent, getting a life, meeting a man to fall in love with. A man like David, perhaps.

David liked her. She liked him. If she went to England, who knew where it would lead?

And then the gate had opened and Lachlan had walked in, and Fiona had known the answer to that: it wouldn't lead anywhere.

She'd already met the man she was in love with—for all the good it did her.

LACHLAN HAD NEVER HAD TO WORK very hard to get a woman's attention. He had certainly never had to compete for it.

And why should he? He was healthy, wealthy, and not half bad looking if the enthusiasm of the women of the world was to be believed.

And that was just the point! There were plenty of bloody women in the world who would be only too happy to be pursued by the likes of Lachlan McGillivray.

But there was only one Fiona Dunbar, damn it to hell.

And all Fiona Dunbar wanted him to do was stand still!

Lachlan didn't want to stand still!

He wanted to grab her and kiss her senseless when she opened the door to him that morning. He wanted to yank her T-shirt over her head instead of shedding his.

He wanted to strip those clay-streaked shorts off her and learn all the secrets of her body—secrets that had been plaguing him ever since the night he'd spent watching her sleep.

And instead here he was, stripping his own shorts off and preparing once more to let her stand there and stare at him. He ground his teeth, caught a glimpse of his wild-eyed countenance in the mirror and drew a quick desperate breath.

Cool it, he told himself and willed his libido into temporary hibernation. Just for now. Just for the moment.

Because this was something he'd agreed to do, he'd do it. He'd see it through as he always saw everything through.

But he was done pretending Fiona could just look her fill with no consequences. This wasn't the academic exercise she was trying to pretend it was.

She could look. She could touch.

But he wanted her naked, too.

"Are you coming?" an impatient voice called through the bathroom door.

Trying not to, Lachlan thought wryly.

"Be right there," he replied, and hoped he didn't sound as ragged as he felt.

When he ambled into the studio a few moments later, Fiona had already set the sculpture on her worktable. It looked a lot different from when he'd left. Much more detailed. She'd done a lot of work on it since he'd been gone. Curious, he went closer to take a look.

"The sooner you get on the stand, the sooner I can get to work," she said, barely glancing his way, rubbing at something on the sculpture's hip.

He studied it, impressed. "You missed me," he said with a grin.

Her gaze jerked up. "What?"

He nodded at the sculpture. "You've been spending a lot of time with him. With me," he added and was pleased to see her cheeks flush.

"I've been working," she said tightly.

"When you weren't schmoozing with Grantham?" He hadn't meant to bring that up. He didn't need her thinking he was jealous of any bloody earl.

"He's been very encouraging," she said and looked from him to the model stand and back again expectantly.

Lachlan took the hint. He padded across the bare floor and got up on the stand. "I'll bet," he muttered.

"He's a nice man," Fiona said absently as she studied him. "I've enjoyed talking with him. I've never met a man quite like him before. Thank you for introducing us."

"I'm a nice man, too," Lachlan pointed out.

"Mmm."

Whatever that meant.

She worked in silence for a while, and Lachlan, silent too, simply watched her.

He'd missed watching her work. He'd expected that once she was out of sight, she'd be out of mind. God knew it was what he'd been hoping for. And with Dooley quitting, it should have been true. He'd had plenty of work at the Sandpiper to occupy him.

And yet all the time he'd been there, he'd felt as if something was missing.

A good contractor, he'd told himself. A competent foreman.

And that was true. But once he'd hired Sylvester, he'd been desperate to get away, to come back to Pelican Cay. Because he couldn't get Fiona Dunbar out of his mind.

And it was nice to see she'd missed him, too. The sculpture was coming right along. Right now, for example, she was adding a chunk of clay to the front of the sculpture below the waist.

Lachlan sucked in his breath. Carefully he swallowed

when Fiona looked up and studied him dispassionately for a long moment, then wet her hands and began using the clay slip to blend the addition in, adding fullness to the groin, smoothing, stroking…

Oh God.

Lachlan shut his eyes. No good. He could still almost feel her hands…

He opened his eyes again and then—

"Hey!" he yelped when she lopped off a piece and dropped it back in the bucket "What the hell did you do that for?"

Fiona looked up, then laughed at his outraged expression. "I used too much."

"Did not," he muttered.

Their gazes caught. Held. Good God she was beautiful. And vibrant. And sexy. Her eyes were wide and luminous. Her skin was golden with freckles and a wonderful all-encompassing blush. He could see a tiny pulse beating at the base of her throat. His gaze dropped to her hands. They were still—and touching the clay intimately.

Lachlan shifted, cleared his throat, cracked a grin. "I hear we're having an affair," he said.

The blush turned as red as her hair. "We're not!"

"I know that," he said drily.

But she didn't even hear him. She was pacing now, waving her hands, color still brilliant in her cheeks. "It's ridiculous! It's because they saw you leaving here in the morning. They think you spent the night!"

"I did."

"No. I mean they think you slept with me!"

"Not a bad idea," he murmured, watching as she went from one side of the room to the other, practically caroming off the walls.

"The whole damn island thinks that I'm your mistress!" She came to a halt directly in front of him and glared.

Lachlan shrugged and grinned. "Now there's an even better idea!"

Fiona punched him in the stomach.

"Hey!" He coughed, then caught his breath, and looked at her closely.

Fiona wasn't looking at him. She had retreated swiftly behind her worktable again and was staring at the sculpture, a shuttered expression on her face.

"Is that a no?" he teased after a moment, wondering what the hell was eating her, trying to get her to smile.

But she didn't smile. She ignored him, focusing intently and completely on the sculpture, using her thumbs to do something to its face.

Smash it in? Lachlan wondered.

"Maybe you could write a letter to the editor denying it?" he suggested lightly. "As I recall you were pretty big on letters to the editor."

"No."

"So, you mean there's hope—" He grinned again.

"Writing a letter wouldn't work. Taking an ad wouldn't work. Believe me, I already considered it."

She had? Being his mistress was that distasteful? Lachlan scowled.

"Don't draw your brows down like that," Fiona said. "I can't get this right if you do."

So he glared at her without drawing his brows down. He frowned and she worked. He fumed and she sculpted until finally she stopped and said, "That's fine. Thanks a lot. You can go."

Like it was dismissal time. Annoyed, Lachlan stalked off and made quick work of getting dressed again. No cold shower necessary this time. Fiona had solved the problem all by herself.

"See you tomorrow," he said as he headed for the stairs. She was standing in the doorway to her studio.

She shook her head. "Not necessary. I'm far enough along now. I don't need to have you model anymore."

He considered that, then cocked his head and said with

a lightness he didn't feel, "You sure? I'm always happy to get naked for you."

If he'd hoped that would help, he was disappointed.

At the sight of his grin, Fiona felt her jaw tighten further. "No thanks. We're done. I'm sure."

THEY WERE FINISHED, just as she'd told him. But the truth was they'd never even really started.

There had never been anything between her and Lachlan McGillivray—not in real life. Only in Fiona's mind and in her heart.

She'd wondered how to tell him about the rumor. She should have known he already knew. She should have known, too, what his reaction would be.

Why not? Great idea! To him it undoubtedly was.

To her it was simply painful because in her heart of hearts she wanted so much more.

And she'd wanted Lachlan to want it, too.

She'd fretted about it all morning. Then she'd got a grip. And now, blinking back stupid tears and grateful for her sunglasses, she marched determinedly up the hill to Carin's shop.

Carin beamed when Fiona came in. "I see Lachlan's back," she said cheerily.

"I saw him comin' from your place this morning," Elaine added with a knowing wink.

Fiona ignored them. "Can I use your computer to send a few e-mails?"

Carin blinked at the lack of reply and the hard tone. "Yes, sure. But—" she paused and looked at Fiona closely. "Are you and Lachlan—"

Fiona gritted her teeth.

"Never mind. None of my business," she said wisely. "None of my business at all." She nodded toward the back room. "You know where it is. Go right ahead."

"Thanks. Will you show me how to do attachments?"

Fiona had had very little reason to e-mail anyone. She'd never sent an attachment in her life.

Today she was going to send four of them.

Carin's brows lifted. "Certainly," she said and followed Fiona into the back room.

"I'm sending out my portfolio," Fiona told her. It was no secret. In fact, the more people who knew, the better. "David helped me get it together last night."

"Portfolio? For what?"

"Art school. He said you might write me a letter of recommendation. He said Nathan might, too."

Carin looked momentarily taken aback. Then she said, "Of course. If that's what you want. Isn't this sudden? Are you sure? Did Lachlan—?"

"This has nothing to do with Lachlan," Fiona snapped. "This has to do with *my* life. Once upon a time I did have one! I had a life before Lachlan McGillivray came back to Pelican Cay."

"Well, yes, but—"

"And it's not sudden. I'd hoped to go to art school years ago before Dad got sick. It's just—it took David to make me see I needed to follow through."

"Of course," Carin said, apparently convinced by her fervency. "I'll certainly recommend you, and I know Nathan will, too. We'll write the letters tonight. But—" she hesitated "—it's awfully late in the year, you know."

"I know," Fiona said. "I need to get started. Will you please show me what to do?"

There were four e-mails to go out with portfolios attached. Applications to the three schools in England that David had recommended. And a fourth to the school in Italy she'd hoped to attend all those years ago.

She couldn't refuse to apply to the English schools. Not after all the help David had given her. But she didn't want to go there if it gave David the wrong idea. She didn't want to lead him on. So she applied to the Italian one as well. It was a good school, emphasizing sculpture. And if once upon a time its geographic proximity to Lachlan had appealed to her, now the attraction was that it was halfway across the world from Pelican Cay.

She typed in the personal application letters she had written out in longhand that morning. Carin helped her attach the files with the photos David had taken of her work. They weren't a lot but they were all—almost all—she had. They would have to do.

She sent them out one after another, then let out a deep breath she didn't even realize she'd been holding.

"All done," she said and stood up. "Thanks." She even managed a smile for Carin and Elaine as she left the shop.

She didn't notice Carin and Elaine going to stand in the window and watch worriedly as she walked back down the street. And she was well out of earshot when Carin said, "I don't know what he did, but I'd like to kick Lachlan McGillivray to Nassau and back."

"MY, YOU'RE UP EARLY." Suzette blinked in surprise when she walked into the office at seven the next morning and found Lachlan already there, poring over some specs for an inn in St Maarten.

"Couldn't sleep," he muttered and tipped back in his desk chair, scowling at the papers in his hand. Couldn't focus on the damn specs, either.

He'd been reading them, trying to make sense of them since five-thirty. He'd awakened, like clockwork at five, had known a moment's eagerness to get up and head over to Fiona's, and then had remembered he wasn't going anymore.

Good, he'd told himself and rolled over to try to go back to sleep. But it hadn't happened. Fifteen minutes of tossing and turning was all he could stand. Then he got up, went for a swim, then came back and got to work. *Tried* to get to work.

He tossed the papers on the desk and stood up. He

needed something more physical. Like tearing down a building.

He went to find his brother.

Hugh, naturally, wasn't up yet.

He squinted blearily when Lachlan walked into his bedroom and jerked open the blinds "What are you doin' here? Wha' time is it? Don't you ever knock?"

"It's seven-thirty. Up and at 'em."

For months Hugh had been trying to get Lachlan to help him tear down the old hut on the land he'd bought beside the cricket field so they could build a machine shop there.

"I've got time now," Lachlan said, kicking the bed frame. "And if you want me to knock, put a lock on your door."

Hugh scowled and pulled the sheet over his head. "Come back when it's morning."

"If I don't go there, I'll dig in here." Looking around at the mess that was his brother's house, Lachlan could almost relish the prospect.

Hugh groaned, then scrubbed his hands through his hair and over his face, and finally hauled himself up. "What's the matter?" he asked. "Fiona kick you out?"

FIONA HAD *NOT* KICKED HIM OUT.

But try telling Hugh that. Or anyone else.

Lachlan understood very quickly the difficulty Fiona had had in convincing anyone that she and he were not having an affair. Everyone on Pelican Cay had their own answers to questions before they even asked.

"What are you doing?" Molly asked when she'd come to work to find Lachlan ripping out a window frame.

"What does it look like?" he growled.

Molly grinned. "Like you're frustrated. Fiona dump you, then?"

"No, damn it. Fiona did *not* dump me!"

But if Hugh and Molly didn't believe it, neither did Carin

or Nathan or Miss Saffron or Maurice and Estelle or any of the kids on his soccer team.

When he yelled at them to pay attention for heaven's sake, they just shook their heads and smiled at each other.

"My aunt dumped him," Peter Dunbar said knowledgeably.

And Lacey Wolfe nodded. "My mother says it must've been something he did."

"Yeah, well," Tom Dunbar dribbled the ball in a circle, "Aunt Fiona doesn't need a boyfriend anyway. She might be goin' to England. Or Italy."

Italy?

"What's with this Italy?" Lachlan demanded.

But the kids didn't know. So he went to the shop and asked Hugh and Molly.

Hugh was as baffled as he was.

But Molly was a woman, even though she was working on Hugh's truck and had a streak of grease on her cheek and a baseball cap on her head. And women apparently understood these things genetically.

"She's applied to art school in Italy. It's where she was hoping to go back before her dad got ill."

"Oh, yeah?" First he'd heard of it. But then, when it came to Fiona, he apparently hadn't heard a lot. "Where in Italy?"

He hadn't heard of the school, but he knew the town. It wasn't a long way from where he'd played soccer.

"When was that?" he said, trying to do the arithmetic.

"Maybe ten, eleven years ago," Molly said.

What if she'd gone to school there when he'd been just down the road? Would he have ever run into her? Would she have come to watch him play?

Had she had any idea he was there?

Probably not, he thought. If she had, she'd have steered clear of Italy! But second thoughts told him just the opposite. She must have known. Molly surely would have told her.

And that meant…

But even at his most egotistical, Lachlan couldn't believe she'd applied to art school in Italy all those years ago because he was playing in goal twenty miles down the road.

He stomped out, kicking the air compressor and almost breaking his toe in the process.

"Cranky, isn't he?" Molly said.

"I would be, too," Hugh said, "if Fiona'd kicked me out."

WITHIN DAYS, Fiona heard on the island telegraph, their affair was over.

"You two didn't last long, did you?" Nikki at the bakery asked. "What'd he do?"

"He didn't hurt you, did he?" Carin demanded.

"I know he's my brother and I know he can be an idiot, and I realize you might not want to tell me," Molly said, "but why did you kick him out?"

Anything she answered, Fiona knew was going to be wrong.

"Lachlan is going his way and I'm going mine," she said. That seemed most diplomatic—and actually closest to the truth.

Or it would have been if Lachlan hadn't started turning up on her doorstep again and again.

The first time she opened the door and found him standing there, a disarming grin on his handsome face, she'd been momentarily speechless. "What are you doing here?" she asked at last.

"You mean you don't want me to strip off my clothes and model for you?" His grin broadened at the sight of her mouth opening and closing like a fish. He shrugged. "Just thought you might like to come to the game today."

"The game?"

"The soccer game," he clarified patiently. "The island team. Boys and girls. The one I'm coaching at your suggestion. I thought you might like to watch us play. That's all."

"Why now?" She hadn't been to a game yet.

"Because you haven't been to a game yet," he said. "And I think the kids would appreciate the support." There was a brief twinkle in his eyes before they got a faraway look.

"'People who are going to take advantage of local amenities,'" he quoted from memory, "'should be willing to contribute their skills— however meager—to the betterment of the island's children.'" He gave her a meaningful look. "Even if it only means you stand there and cheer."

"Yes, I…I see what you mean. I'll…do that. Sometime. Not now. I have work to do now." She started to close the door.

"Got a new naked guy in the studio?"

"I'm doing Lacey Wolfe. Fully clothed."

He grinned. "Glad to hear it. Well, another time then," he gave her a wink and bounded off the porch leaving her staring after him.

He stopped by late that evening to tell her about the game. "Thought you'd want to know we won," he said and walked straight past her without an invitation and went into the kitchen where he opened the refrigerator, took out the jug and poured them each a glass of iced tea. Then he paced the room, glass in hand, describing the game in vivid detail.

Fiona huddled against the counter, clutching Sparks in her arms, as she feasted her eyes on him at the same time she wished desperately that he would go away!

"Your nephew Tom, he's a good player. You should have come to watch him."

"I couldn't."

"Next time then."

"We'll see." She hugged Sparks tighter as Lachlan leaned back against the counter and made no move to leave. "Why are you doing this?" she asked him at last. "The 'affair' business was dying down. It was over! And now here you are again.''

"Maybe I'm hoping."

"Well, stop hoping!"

He shook his head slowly. "No."

Over the next week he turned up relentlessly. He stopped in at Carin's shop when she was working. He ate at the bakery when she was waiting tables. He followed along when she was out at low tide looking for material for *The King of the Beach*.

Fiona did her best to remain polite but distant.

She sold him trinkets at Carin's. She poured his coffee at the bakery and declined the offer to share his key lime pie. She said somewhat testily that if he was going to follow her while she was scavenging he could make himself useful and carry things for her.

"Sure," he said and held out his arms.

So she loaded him down with whatever she found and worked intently in an effort not to notice him.

With water-torture-like patience Lachlan persisted.

"Don't you have work to do?" Fiona demanded.

Lachlan nodded. "I'm doing what it takes to succeed," he told her gravely and kept right on turning up in her life.

To succeed? At what?

The answer was obvious. He wanted her in his bed.

And every day Fiona hoped desperately that she would get word from one of the schools she'd applied to. She didn't know how much longer she could resist.

A LESSER MAN would have thrown in the towel.

A week went by, then two, then three. He stopped by her house, invited her along to games or to dinner, made it a point to stop and watch every day as she worked on her beloved *King of the Beach*. He even made himself useful lugging stuff she found that washed up on the tide.

And while she never gave him any obvious encouragement, every now and then Lachlan felt a ray of hope.

He'd give her credit for stubbornness. She was doing her best to ignore him. But that was just the point. If she'd treated him with the casual ease she treated all the other guys on the island—even Lord Bloody Grantham before he'd gone back to England, thank God, last week—Lachlan might have worried.

But she didn't.

She got a little rigid and flustered whenever he came around. And he'd seen her watching him on the beach, at the bar, playing soccer—after his needling, she had actually come to a game or two—when she thought he didn't notice.

He noticed.

Lachlan had spent his life noticing tiny things that tipped him off to how the other team was going to play the ball. Over the years he'd honed his instincts well. Now he dared to hope she wasn't quite as indifferent as she pretended to be.

But at the rate she was going, they'd be old and gray before he ever even managed to kiss her again!

Sometimes even the goalkeeper had to go on offense. Sometimes a guy had to make things happen, had to take a risk.

CHAPTER EIGHT

"I SAW SOMETHING up at Eden Cove the other day that you might want to use for your sculpture."

Fiona looked down from astride the driftwood spar torso of *The King of the Beach* to see Lachlan squinting up at her.

"Eden Cove?" Fiona echoed cautiously. She was attaching a black plastic lid eye patch that had floated in on last night's tide. She wanted to concentrate on it. But Eden Cove was the most beautiful place she knew. A tiny perfect cove on the seaward side of nearby uninhabited Isla Seca, accessible only by boat, it was often the setting for tropical paradise photo shoots.

Deserted, it was a place for lovers.

Fiona had never been there with a lover. But she'd had her share of dreams and fantasies, many of them featuring Lachlan McGillivray and herself.

"I don't think so," she said after a moment's reflection.

"Your loss." Lachlan shrugged. He reached out and patted one of the sculpture's driftwood legs. "Too bad, ol' buddy." He turned and began to walk away.

"What sort of something," Fiona called after him before she could stop herself.

He turned back and shaded his eyes with his hand as he looked up again. "Fishing net."

Fiona couldn't stop her eyes growing round and eager. A fishing net would be a perfect addition, the finishing touch bringing it all together. There was so much she could do with a fishing net.

She'd been tempted more than once to use one of her dad's. But from the beginning, everything she'd used had come in on the tide. Even the red bikini bottoms that had brought Lachlan, furious, to her door had fortuitously washed up on the beach. It was a rule she'd made when she'd begun. To use anything that hadn't washed up would be cheating.

"What sort of fishing net?" she asked cautiously, determinedly tempering her enthusiasm.

If he thought that was a stupid question from a fisherman's daughter, he didn't say so. "Pretty big from the looks of it," he told her. "It's mostly buried in the sand. Looks pretty old. Maybe you wouldn't be interested." He started to turn away again.

"And you just...just left it there?"

He looked back. "Of course I left it there. Why would I want an old fishing net? I just thought you might. If you don't..."

"I do," she said quickly before she could stop herself. Then she swallowed and tried to look casual. "I might," she corrected. "I'll check it out."

Lachlan nodded. "I'll take you. Pick you up tomorrow morning about ten." And before she could object, he sauntered off whistling, leaving Fiona to stare after him.

IN THE MORNING the weather was gorgeous, hot but not sticky, a few puffy clouds, and the wind was light.

"A perfect day for a sail," Carin said when Fiona appeared at the shop to drop off some sand castles the next morning. "You'll have a grand time."

She knew Fiona was going with Lachlan this morning. She knew why. There would be no more "island telegrams" confusing things where she and Lachlan were concerned.

"I'm not going for a good time. I'm going for the net," Fiona said firmly.

Carin began unpacking the sand castles. "Well, my best

guess is you'll have a good time *and* you'll get a net. Go on. Have fun. Enjoy. It's a gorgeous day. Smile.''

Fiona smiled. Faintly. She felt vaguely worried. Apprehensive. If Lachlan made one wrong move…

But when Lachlan came to get her, she couldn't fault him. He was prompt, cheerful, courteous. A regular Boy Scout, Fiona thought, and tried to scowl as she accompanied him down the quay to the dock.

But it was difficult because it was, as Carin had said, a fantastic day.

Having grown up around fishing boats, Fiona was used to being on the water. But she'd always been ballast while her brothers ran things. Boats were ''guy stuff'' and her involvement was not welcome.

She had never sailed in a sailboat in her life.

So she stayed out of the way while Lachlan warmed up the throaty diesel engine, untied and coiled the lines, then backed the boat out of the slip. Then, turning the boat into the wind, he adjusted the throttle so they were moving slowly, and motioned her over, then put her at the helm. ''Keep it heading dead into the wind while I hoist the main.''

Fiona looked at him in momentary wide-eyed panic. She'd never been allowed to take the wheel when her brothers were around. But Lachlan seemed to think it was no big deal. He didn't even pay any attention to what she was doing, instead moving forward to raise the mainsail.

Basking in his confidence, Fiona eased her death grip on the wheel slightly and took a deep breath as the boat churned steadily ahead and Lachlan cranked up the mainsail. Then he cleated off the halyard and stowed the winch handle before coming her way again.

She started to move aside, but he shook his head. ''Stay there,'' he said, ''and steer for the point while I unfurl the jib.''

Surprised, Fiona did as she was told. She turned the wheel so they were headed slightly off the wind, a smile lighting her face as Lachlan unfurled the jib. The sails caught the wind and the boat began to pick up speed.

Yes! she thought. Oh, yes!

Then Lachlan cut the engine. And the sudden silence, broken only by the slap and hiss of water against the hull, startled her so that she laughed delightedly.

Lachlan cocked his head. "What?"

"Nothing. Everything. This is…it's marvelous." She beamed. "Sailing is, I mean. I never knew."

"Never knew? You've never sailed?" Now it was his turn to look amazed. "But your dad—Mike and Paul—"

"My dad fished. My brothers fish. Dunbars spend their lives in boats. But for them boats are business, not pleasure. And they never let me do anything," she admitted. "Some fishermen think women on boats are bad luck."

Lachlan looked as if she'd just uttered a sacrilege. But then he grinned and shook his head, his dark hair lifting in the breeze. "You don't look like bad luck to me."

And just for an instant, when Lachlan's eyes—as deep and blue as the sea—met hers, Fiona's heart kicked over. Quickly she looked away, started to get up to move. But he blocked her in.

"Stay put. Go ahead and sail her."

"I can't."

"Sure you can." He moved behind her and put his hands over hers, and Fiona's breath caught in her chest, but she didn't object.

They sailed up the coast and past the point. Then he taught her how to come about, turning through the eye of the wind while he brought the jib around and retrimmed the sails.

When they reached the cove he had her steer again while he lowered the sails and started the engine. The noise seemed almost deafening, and Fiona was glad when he cut the engine again and lowered the anchor, then backed off the boat to set it about fifty yards from the shore.

Eden Cove with its narrow sandy beach, crystal clear

water and ring of coconut palms was every bit as beautiful as she remembered. It looked like the cover illustration for a romance.

"It certainly captures the mood," Julie had once said with a smile after she'd been there with Paul.

"The blue lagoon," Claire had agreed. "For real."

Fiona knew plenty of guys who had brought girls to Eden Cove. And she wondered again if there really was a net—or if Lachlan had designs of his own. She shot a quick look at him to see if she could read his mind.

He was scanning the shoreline. "We can take the dinghy in from here or swim. What's your pleasure?" He sounded perfectly matter-of-fact and Fiona knew it was her own heated imagination that was creating the problems here, not Lachlan's.

"Swim," Fiona said. A cool dunk in the ocean seemed a smart idea.

Before she could feel self-conscious about stripping off her shirt and shorts, Lachlan said, "Race you," pulled his own T-shirt over his head, kicked his flip-flops off, and dove over the side.

Seconds later Fiona had stripped down to her navy-blue swimsuit and dove in after him.

Lachlan swam like he played soccer and sailed and swung a hammer and tore down buildings, with easy grace and competence. Doing a leisurely breast stroke so she could watch him, Fiona wondered if there was anything physical he didn't do well.

She wondered how he made love.

Oh God. She sank beneath the surface and didn't come up until she'd controlled her wayward brain again.

And when she got to a depth where she could stand, the first thing she said was, "Where's the net?"

"Here," Lachlan said, and moved a few feet up the beach, then crouched down and began digging at something with his hands.

By the time Fiona waded ashore, she could see he was

dragging an old fisherman's net out from where most of it had been buried beneath the sand.

"Oh, wow!" She grinned with delight as she ran through the water and up the sand to help him dig. "Is that a float, too?"

It was, indeed. A pale-green glass float was still attached. Carefully, Fiona dug around it, then lifted it and cradled it in her palm. "Oh, it's lovely!"

"Your brothers probably have a slew of them."

"But this one washed up on the beach," Fiona said, giving him a brilliant smile. "This one is special."

He looked amused, but he didn't argue and he helped her dig the rest of the net out.

It had been ripped badly and the ends of the strands were frayed and torn. Not even the most dedicated old fisherman would mend it now, but as she ran her fingers over the mesh she could almost imagine the man who had used it day in and day out—a man like her father, a man of the sea.

Holding the net in her lap, she lifted her gaze to meet Lachlan's. "It's perfect," she told him. "Thank you. Thank you so much."

He looked almost embarrassed at her sincerity. He shrugged awkwardly and looked away, then got to his feet and brushed the sand off his legs. "No problem. I just figured you might be able to use it."

"I can use it," she said softly, smiling up at him.

"Yeah, well, good." He cracked his knuckles. "I'm getting hungry. I'll swim out to the boat and put in the raft and bring back lunch."

"Lunch?" she said, surprised.

But Lachlan had already sprinted into the water and was swimming toward the boat. While he was gone, she gathered up the net and carried it into the water, then spread it out, rinsed it and folded it. She had washed the float as well by the time Lachlan returned in the dinghy.

He had a picnic hamper with him and an old blanket that

he carried ashore and spread out beneath what shade there was from the brush and the palms. Then, as Fiona watched, he opened the hamper and began setting out containers of food.

"Conch salad," he said as he set one down and then another. "Jerk chicken. Coconut shrimp. Breadfruit chips. Mango salsa—"

"Lachlan! What on earth? Where did you get all that?"

"Maddie made it." She was the cook at the Moonstone. "I asked her for something to take along in case we got hungry."

"And she sent a feast?" Fiona was flabbergasted.

"She's practicing," Lachlan said. "Come on. Sit down and dig in." He was putting out plates and silverware as he spoke. "We're experimenting with providing picnic lunches for the guests," he told her. "Seeing what works. Consider yourself a guinea pig." He grinned at her.

"A guinea pig, my foot," Fiona muttered. But she sat. She was hungry. Sailing had made her hungry. Being out in the fresh air, swimming, digging in the sand—all of it— made her ravenous. So she ate.

It was wonderful. All of it. Lachlan opened a beer and offered her one, but she took a pineapple soda instead, then followed his lead and stretched out casually on the blanket.

And they talked.

He asked her about her sculpting and she told him what she was working on now. She asked him about the Sandpiper and he told her about the progress they were making there.

"It's been a challenge, but I'd enjoy it more if I were doing it myself instead of having to hire it done."

"Why don't you do it?"

"Because I have things that keep me on Pelican Cay," he said. "That's why I like helping Hugh. I like banging with hammers," he confessed. "I've never minded getting my hands dirty."

And this was true, she realized. He had never simply

thrown money into the restorations and renovations he had done on the Moonstone. And if he wasn't doing the actual work on the Sandpiper and his other inns, he still, she was sure, had a hand in every decision, a finger in every pie.

He was a stickler for detail. That's what he'd been doing on Eden when he found the net, he told her.

"I had heard there might be some good fieldstone back in the bush. We've been looking for some for the fireplaces. So I thought I'd check it out."

"That's why you were here?" Fiona asked, she looked up from drawing in the sand and slanted him a quick glance.

"That's why," Lachlan said. He looked her square in the eyes. "I didn't bring anyone else here."

"I wasn't asking!" Fiona protested, though she couldn't deny her relief at his words. She felt better. Happier. She smiled at him.

He smiled at her.

The sun beat down on her back. Perspiration trickled between her breasts. She could hear the blood pounding in her veins, and her heart thudding loudly in her chest.

"Swim?" Lachlan said and in one fluid movement rose to his feet. He held out a hand to her.

Nerveless, Fiona put out hers and he drew her to her feet. They stood there inches apart. She could see the individual grains of sand against the tan of his hair-roughened chest.

"C'mon," he said, his voice husky. And, fingers still laced with hers, he drew her with him into the water.

They swam together lazily, out to the boat and around it, using sidestrokes so that their gazes locked and they could speak.

But they didn't speak. They swam in wordless communion, their movements synchronized. And every now and then Fiona felt the brush of Lachlan's foot on her calf or hers on his leg. They were fleeting touches. Nothing, really. And yet with every second her awareness grew, her breathing quickened, her sensitivity increased until even the feel of the water slipping over her made her tingle with anticipation.

"Want to build a sand castle?" Lachlan asked suddenly, his voice sounding ragged to her ears.

Fiona blinked and nearly sank. Build a sand castle? But—

But then she drew a shaky breath and nodded. She put a damper on her anticipation. But it didn't go away. It was still there. Like a banked fire, it warmed her more than the afternoon sun as they sprawled on the sand and built a castle.

Lachlan moved energetically and with purpose. Fiona moved languidly, still feeling the heat of desire. It smoldered as she watched Lachlan's strong arms digging and pressing and molding the sand, as she admired the hard muscles in his tanned calves and thighs as he crouched and shifted, as she studied the curve of his spine and his broad back and well-defined shoulders.

And the fire sparked to life again every time Lachlan's eyes met hers.

"Hey, how come I'm doing all the work?" he asked, grinning and flicking the hair off his forehead.

"I'm the contractor," Fiona told him. "And you don't mind getting your hands dirty."

"You don't either," he reminded her. "All that clay."

She remembered her hands in the clay, remembered them sculpting his body. She'd finished that piece finally a few days ago. And she'd done a pretty good job if she did say so herself. Of course, she'd had a lot of inspiration!

Her gaze roved over him now.

"Okay, that's it! Enough castle." Lachlan jumped to his feet and, grabbing her hand, ran with her into the water, only letting go when he dove beneath the surface.

On fire now, Fiona ran with him and dove, too.

And when they came up, Lachlan kissed her.

It was a gentle kiss. Asking, not demanding. If it had

been demanding, she could have resisted, her defenses would have saved her.

But she had no defense against his gentleness. Against him.

Not any longer. He'd got under her defenses. He'd made her love him.

She kissed him back. She touched him, running her hands over his arms and shoulders and down his hard wet back.

And he touched her.

It was everything Fiona ever dreamed of and more. Her fantasies had been wonderful. Reality was so much more.

The kiss that began as a gentle question within seconds became a demanding conflagration. His hands were learning her curves, making her tremble. Her body was turning to quivering jelly. And Lachlan's was turning to steel.

And then he lifted her and carried her out of the water up to the blanket on the beach under the palms where he gently laid her down. Then kneeling beside her, he ran his hands over her. She could feel the fine tremor in his fingers and smiled at the knowledge that he was affected, too.

And then there was no more reflection, no more thinking. Only feeling. Only touching.

Her swimsuit vanished. His trunks disappeared. And feverishly she explored his body with her hands, learning through them what the clay had only approximated. When she sculpted, the clay felt alive.

But not like this.

Clay was not hot the way Lachlan was hot. It never grew under her touch, never responded as eagerly as the man did, his muscles tensing, his whole body growing taut, the breath hissing between his teeth.

"You're killing me," he muttered, his desperate fingers learning her slickness, her secrets.

Fiona gasped, then shuddered, her body straining for his. "Now, Lachlan! Now!"

She reached for him, grabbing his hips as he slid hard

and full inside her. "Yes," she said, reveling in it, at the same time sensing that it wasn't enough.

And then he began to move.

They were too hot, too hungry, too desperate. It couldn't last.

Didn't.

It built and built and built. And then it exploded, a fire-ball, Fiona thought. As much as she could muster any thoughts at all.

And yet after, with Lachlan spent and trembling in her arms, she didn't feel shattered at all. She felt like a piece of her sculpture that had been through the fire of the kiln. Tested. Fired. Finished.

Made whole.

She smiled into his shoulder. She pressed light kisses along the line of his jaw. With her fingers she drew lazy circles on his sun-warmed back, walked them down his spine, over his buttocks. Hard buttocks, she thought, squeezing experimentally.

"You're asking for trouble," Lachlan mumbled against her cheek.

"Am I?" Fiona said hopefully, fingers moving.

He rolled off her and laughed, looking younger and happier than she had ever seen him. "Give me a few minutes," he vowed, "and you'll find out."

A few minutes later she found out he was right.

This time when they made love it was with slow, leisurely thoroughness that left them both sated and satisfied—for the moment.

And when they sailed home that evening, with the net and float tucked securely away, Fiona stood at the wheel with Lachlan's arms around her and marveled at the fact that, sometimes, dreams really did come true.

CHAPTER NINE

IT WAS WELL AFTER DARK by the time they got back to the harbor.

Fiona, hugging the net to her chest, watched as Lachlan secured the boat. Then, when he scrambled up on the dock and held out a hand to her, she let him pull her up beside him.

Fingers laced together, they walked up the dock and along the quay. Half a dozen teenagers were hanging out under the streetlamps, laughing and talking, and as Fiona and Lachlan passed, they turned and watched.

So much for shutting down the island telegraph. Fiona had no doubt but that the island telegraph would be working overtime tonight. She didn't care.

They reached her door and Lachlan said quietly, "Can I come in?" and she knew it was reality time, not fantasy time any longer.

She'd never actually dared dream of having Lachlan in her own bed. But the net in her arms told her he understood her, the day on the island said she mattered, and the look in his eyes was impossible to resist.

She kissed his cheek, took his hand and drew him in.

SHE WAS AS FIERY AS HER HAIR.

He'd known she would be and relished every minute as, defenses battered down at last, she came to him as wild and strong as the sea.

He'd worried that once he brought her home the idyll would end and the walls would go up again. He rejoiced when instead she kissed him, when she opened her door to him, when she brought him upstairs to her bedroom, when they undressed each other slowly, stopping to touch, to kiss, to stroke, and when they lay together on her narrow bed and loved each other once more.

He loved the way she met him every step of the way, move for move, touch for touch, kiss for kiss. He loved the way he could make her writhe and arch and lock her heels against the backs of his thighs and sob his name. He loved the way she could make him bite his lip with longing, could make him quiver with need, and could satisfy both in the warmth of her embrace.

He loved her once, twice. They fell asleep in each other's arms and woke twice more to love again.

And when at dawn Lachlan woke to find Fiona in the curve of his arm, her legs tangled with his, her lips pressed against his chest, more than anything, he wanted her again.

But she didn't wake this time as he shifted and eased his leg from between hers. She sighed and slept on when he levered himself up on an elbow to look down at her.

Her hair was fire against the pillow, strands glowing red and copper in the streaky dawn. Her lips were full and slightly parted, asking to be kissed yet again.

And he kissed them lightly, willing her to wake, but he had worn her out, and so she slept. He stroked her hair, touched her cheek. Still she slept. And so he kissed her again gently, then reluctantly got out of bed.

He had to go back to the Sandpiper this morning. He had to see what Sylvester had done. Then there was a lunch meeting in Nassau with his banker, and then more meetings with more investors to go over a proposal for his next acquisition. He didn't want to do any of them. He wanted to stay in bed with Fiona.

But he couldn't. And he knew she couldn't either.

She worked at the bakery at lunch. She'd be at Carin's this afternoon. But she would be home this evening. And if he got moving now, so would he. He dressed quickly, then wrote her a note.

He wasn't good with words, had always wished he could be better. He simply told it like it was. "Fiona," he wrote, "it was the best day—and night—of my life. Back tonight. Love, Lachlan."

He propped it on the nightstand, touched her cheek for just a moment, then scratched Sparks behind the ears, went down the stairs. The net and the float were lying on the sofa where Fiona had left them before they'd come upstairs.

Lachlan spared them a grateful glance, then let himself out the door and hurried up the road.

FIONA SANG HER WAY through the morning.

She could have wished to wake up with Lachlan still there. But he had been there; she hadn't dreamed it.

She had the note to prove it, had found it the moment she awoke, alone and oddly lonely in her bed. Then she had remembered and rolled over, feeling bereft, to find the paper leaning against her reading lamp. She picked it up and smiled at Lachlan's spiky writing, gloried at his words.

It had been the best day and night of her life, too.

And "Love, Lachlan," he had written.

Love.

Fiona grinned and hugged herself. He might not have said it yet, but he had written the word.

Then she sighed and stretched and felt her body protest, aching as it did in mysterious intimate ways in which her body was not accustomed to aching. She ran her hands over her nakedness. Then sat up, energized, excited, and bounded out of bed. She laughed as she dressed, picked up Sparks and danced around the room with him.

He muttered a very offended feline protest.

But Fiona just smiled and danced on.

She didn't exactly dance and sing as she waited on her lunchtime customers. But she was obviously a little ray of sunshine because Tony said, "You should smile like that more often," and she got extraordinarily big tips.

She charmed all the tourists who came into Carin's shop that afternoon, too. She sold several sand castles, two cut-out metal surfers and one fisherman, several wooden fish mobiles, a children's puzzle, a watercolor seascape of Carin's and several of Nathan's books.

By the time Carin and Nathan stopped in at the end of the day, the shelves were looking a little bare.

Carin raised her brows. "Were we ransacked?"

Fiona shook her head, still smiling broadly. "We just had a bunch of tourists with lots of discretionary income today."

"It be on account of her smilin' so much," Miss Saffron said. She had brought over some straw hats she'd made, and now she regarded Fiona with a satisfied smile of her own. "My Letitia, she say she see this one walking hip to hip with that McGillivray boy las' night."

Carin's brows went even higher. "Ah. So you did have a good time then?" she said to Fiona.

Miss Saffron snickered. "Oh my, did she!"

Fiona flushed. "We had a good time."

"And got the net?" Carin said.

"And got the net," Fiona affirmed. "I'm putting it up as soon as I get finished here."

"Well, don't let us keep you," Carin said, making shooing motions with her hands. "You'll want to have it up by the time Lachlan gets back."

The soccer team was out practicing on the field when Fiona arrived. She could see her nephews, Peter and Tom, passing a ball back and forth, dribbling down the field. Lacey Wolfe was practicing with them, too. And Lorenzo Sawyer was crouched, Lachlan-like, in goal.

Lachlan, of course, wasn't there. But she could certainly see his influence. The kids worked purposefully, kicking and passing, heading and blocking, encouraging each other.

They were so much better at the game now, so much more skillful than they ever used to be.

Hitching the net and float over her shoulder, she clambered up *The King.* Then, straddling one of the spars, she attached the float to a fish line and hung it, then began to arrange the net.

"Hey, lookin' good," came a voice from below.

And Fiona glanced down to see Hugh grinning her way. He wore flip-flops and shorts and a disreputable T-shirt, and his dark hair, so like his brother's, lifted in the breeze.

"What are you doing here? I thought you were with Lachlan."

"I had to use the chopper to take Wilson to Governor's Harbour for a meeting. Molly took Lachlan in the plane. They ought to be back before dusk. She radioed in an hour or so ago." He winked. "Bet you can hardly wait."

Fiona flushed, but didn't deny it.

"Glad you and Lachlan are working things out," Hugh went on.

"Me, too," she agreed, and continued to hang the net. "Isn't this perfect?"

"Yep. Looks great." Hugh shaded his eyes and watched her work. "Trust Lachlan to find a use for his old net."

Fiona went suddenly still. Her fingers tightened in the mesh and slowly she turned to look down at Hugh. "What did you say? What do you mean, *his* old net?"

Hugh shrugged. "Well, it wasn't his originally, but he caught it the first year we came here. Maurice took us fishing off Lubbock Point. Lachlan didn't want to go. Too busy sulking. But Dad insisted. It was part of his 'getting to love the island' scheme. Dad caught a shark, I caught a barracuda, and Lachlan caught that old net." Hugh laughed at the memory. "He was furious. Said it figured. That it was just an example of what a dead-end place this was." He shook his head. "Reckon he doesn't think so anymore." He grinned and looked up at Fiona for agreement.

Fiona couldn't manage a word.

"Wondered why he stopped by the other night lookin' for it," Hugh went on cheerfully. "Good idea, really, giving it to you. No sense in keepin' it in the bottom of the closet forever. You can't catch anything with a net like that."

On the contrary, Fiona thought grimly, he had caught her.

THE SUN WAS JUST SETTING as they landed.

"Happy now?" Molly asked as the plane bobbed in the water and she shut things down.

"Yeah," Lachlan said, scanning the dock for Fiona. He'd been distracted and twitchy all day, preoccupied with thoughts of her. He'd have called her while he was at the Sandpiper, but by the time he'd had a spare minute, he knew she would have already headed off to the bakery.

When he had another chance just before Molly had taken him to Nassau for a meeting at the bank, he knew she'd still be serving lunches. And the entire afternoon, when he might have caught her at Carin's, he was tied up with examining a property that had just come on the market. He'd ground his teeth and cracked his knuckles and tried to look attentive and interested. He just wanted to get home to her.

He'd met Molly at the airport, eager to leave, and was annoyed when his sister suggested staying in Nassau for the night to watch a tennis tournament, then maybe catch a movie.

"No reason to hurry back, is there?"

"Yes," Lachlan had said through his teeth. "Let's go."

"Got a hot date, bro?" she'd teased.

He'd considered telling her to mind her own business, then changed his mind. What happened between him and Fiona was Molly's business because it was real. It was serious. It was going to last.

And so he nodded. "That's right."

Molly's eyes had widened and she'd stared at him, as if unsure whether or not he was kidding.

He stared her down.

"Whoa," she said happily after a long moment. Then she'd hustled him to the plane. "Gotta get you home."

And now they were home. And as he climbed into the raft he could see there were half a dozen people on the dock. But no Fiona.

Of course, he thought, lips twitching, she could be at home waiting for him in bed. He could handle that.

But before he could get off the raft, Suzette came purposefully toward him.

"Good. You're back," she said and started in with a list as long as his arm of things he needed to do at once.

"It can't wait?"

"I wouldn't be here if it could."

Better to get them done now, so she wasn't bothering him later. No one was going to bother him and Fiona later.

Sparing a lingering wishful glance across the water at Fiona's house, he allowed Suzette to whisk him off to the Moonstone.

He tried calling Fiona on the way, but she didn't answer.

"Let's get this over with," he said to Suzette, his mind still on Fiona. Maybe she was at one of her brothers' places. Or maybe she'd gone to the Grouper with Carin and Nathan. He tried calling again. There was no reply.

It was almost eleven by the time he had all the letters signed, all the questions answered, all the issues resolved.

"That it?" he asked the minute Suzette showed any signs of slowing down.

"I think so." She stifled a yawn. "Good night. See you in the morning."

Lachlan was already heading for the door. It was late, he knew. Fiona might already have gone to bed. Maybe he should stay home, go see her in the morning. But even as he thought it, he knew he wasn't going to. He'd spent the day thinking of Fiona and missing her. He wasn't spending the night that way, too.

He wanted her to know he'd been thinking of her. In the

ten minutes he'd had free today he'd dropped into a book shop and bought her a book on sculpture. He wanted to take it to her now.

He held it out eagerly when she finally opened the door. She didn't smile. She looked as if she'd been crying.

Lachlan's own smile faded. "What's wrong?"

Fiona stared at him, then took the book and flung it in his face.

Instinctively he dodged. It hit him in the shoulder and thudded on to the porch. "What the hell—? What's the matter with you?"

"I'm a damn fool, obviously!" She started to slam the door, but he caught it before she could and pushed inside as she whirled away from him.

"Look, I'm sorry I wasn't here this morning. I had meetings. I—"

"I'm sorry you were here last night! I'd say what kind of fool do you take me for—but you were obviously right! Are you collecting blue swimsuits now?"

He shook his head, baffled. *"What?"*

"Just get out. Take your stupid net—the one you *found* at Eden Cove—and shove it—"

Oh, hell.

He should have known.

Damn Hugh anyway. Because she had to have talked to Hugh. Why the hell hadn't he told his brother to keep his mouth shut? But then, it wasn't really Hugh's fault, either.

It was his own.

He should have straightened that out last night. He should have told her.

Now Lachlan raked a hand through his hair. "Look," he said with all the reason he could manage. "I know you're upset—"

"Upset?" Fiona shouted. "I'm not upset! I'm bloody furious! How dare you *pretend* to have found that net—"

"I *did* find the net!"

"You *snagged* the net twenty years ago! Off Lubbock Point! Which is *not* near Eden Cove!"

"It's all the same ocean! For heaven's sake, Fiona, I found it in the *ocean!* The same ocean all the other trash came out of. I didn't buy it or steal it or make it. What difference does it make whether I found it now or twenty years ago?"

"It makes all the difference in the world!" she told him flatly. "And you know it does—or you wouldn't have lied about it."

Which was unfortunately true.

Her back was ramrod straight as she stalked to the end of the living room, then spun around to confront him. "And then there's the little matter of where. Why Eden Cove, Lachlan? If it was only to get me to use a net you knew I wouldn't use unless it washed up on the beach, why not say you saw it on our beach. Why go all the way to Eden Cove?"

Well, they both knew why.

Because ultimately this wasn't about the net.

It had been about the two of them.

Nothing that had happened yesterday would have been possible if he'd "found" the net on the beach outside the Moonstone. There was no privacy on the beach outside the Moonstone. There was no fantasy there. There would have been no romantic idyll. No chance to make love to her. No chance that she would have fallen in love with him.

"It gave us a chance," Lachlan tried to tell her.

"It gave you a chance to take advantage of me," she spat.

"I wasn't—"

"Go to hell," she snapped. "You got what you wanted. Get out of here. Get out of my life."

"Fiona! Listen to me!"

"No! Go! Damn you!" She was blinking furiously, close to tears.

He wanted to reach for her, to pull her close and hold her. But when he moved closer, she kicked him.

"Get out! Now!" And she snatched up a large towel-wrapped object and thrust it into his arms. "And take your naked self with you before I smash it to smithereens!"

HE TOOK IT.

He went. He stalked home across the island, as furious as she was, not caring who'd heard them shouting, not caring who'd seen him leave. He was angry, damn it all.

And he'd been misunderstood!

He'd done what he'd done because it had been the only way to break the impasse. She'd turned down every other invitation he'd given her. She'd ignored every overture.

What was he supposed to do?

Besides, it wasn't as if she didn't want to make love with him. She'd been as eager—as desperate—as he had. It hadn't been all one-sided, that was for sure!

And it wasn't as if it was all physical, either. He'd thought about her damn sculpture, hadn't he? He'd given her the net because he took her sculpture seriously.

She'd realize that when she came to her senses.

He'd left the book lying on the porch. She could find it in the morning when, God willing, she was rational again. She could pick it up and recognize that he had always had her best interests at heart.

Then she could come and apologize to him!

SHE DIDN'T APOLOGIZE.

A week went by and he didn't hear a word from her.

He heard a lot from everyone else on the island. Everywhere he went people wanted to know what happened between them.

"I gave her a net I found," he said. "She got upset. That's it."

"That's not exactly the way I heard it," his sister Molly said flatly. "I heard you used it to get what you wanted."

"That's not true."

Once, it might have been.

Back when Fiona had been "the one that got away," when he'd been attracted by her long legs and fiery hair, getting her into bed had been his goal. But somewhere along the line the legs and hair were only part of what attracted him to Fiona.

He'd made love to her on the beach and in her bedroom. He'd made love to her fiercely and passionately, he'd made love to her slowly and tenderly. But he knew now that he could make love to her a hundred times in a hundred places in a hundred different ways, and it would never be enough.

Because he wanted not simply to make love to Fiona, but to talk to Fiona, to walk with Fiona. He wanted to argue with her and laugh with her. He wanted to make up with her. He wanted not just to go to bed with her, but to wake up in the morning next to Fiona, to come home to her in the evenings. He want to spend the rest of his life with her.

He had never really thought in terms of lifetimes before.

He was a man with a ninety-minute attention span, according to the press. He had certainly never thought in terms of marriage, in terms of forever. Not with any woman—let alone Fiona Dunbar.

But now he was thinking about it, and he had to make her understand. He loved her. And she loved him, damn it!

He knew it. And not only because of the day they'd spent at Eden Cove and the night they'd shared the bed—and their bodies—in her bedroom. He knew it because of the way she sometimes looked at him, because of the way she listened to him, and smiled at him. He knew it because of the sculpture she'd made of him.

It was him in the altogether, no doubt about that—Lachlan McGillivray, exposed.

But he wasn't the only one exposed.

Fiona had exposed herself, too. She had used her considerable talent to sculpt him with both passion and compassion. In his terra-cotta likeness he could see strength and determination, power and intensity, vision and idealism, hope and promise.

She had taken the best of him and given it form. She had seen him and sculpted him with eyes of love.

He knew it. And he was sure she knew it—which was why she'd thrust the sculpture into his arms to get rid of it. She hadn't wanted to face that love.

"Well, you'd better tell her fast," Molly said bluntly. "Because she's leaving."

"What the hell do you mean, she's leaving?"

"Going to art school, remember? I saw her at the post office. She got the letter back today."

Oh, hell. She couldn't. She wouldn't!

But he knew Fiona. She was just that stubborn.

HE BANGED ON HER DOOR for the fourth time, then paced the length of the porch and banged again.

"She be in there," her next-door neighbor Carlotta had told him cheerfully when he'd come up the street. "You be goin' to make up with her? Say you sorry?"

He was going to say what needed to be said—if she'd open the damn door.

He banged again. "I know you're in there, Fiona," he shouted. "And I'm not leaving, so you might as well open the door."

Watching avidly from her porch swing. Carlotta gave him a silent round of applause.

He did *not* want an audience. But clearly Carlotta wasn't abandoning the best seat in the house. In fact, he could see Miss Saffron making her way down the street as fast as her old legs could shuffle. He groaned and shut his eyes.

The door creaked.

His eyes snapped open again.

Fiona stood in the doorway, hanging on to the door, making it very clear she was not about to let him in. She still looked pale and shattered, and he wanted to take her in his arms, but knew he had to say things first.

"We need to talk."

"No," she said. "We don't."

"I need to make things clear."

"Things are clear." Her voice was only slightly reedy. "You clarified them beautifully."

"I didn't mean—"

"Regardless of what you meant," she continued ruthlessly, "you made me realize that there are some dreams worth pursuing and some that were kid stuff and better left behind."

"Which means what? That you're leaving? Molly said you got a letter. What are you going to do, just going to turn your back on what's between us? Just go to England or Italy or wherever and pretend it simply doesn't exist?"

"I would if I could," Fiona replied tonelessly, "but I didn't get accepted. I'll have to think of something else."

And she closed the door in his face.

FIONA HAD ALWAYS KNOWN that art school was a long shot.

But she'd had some encouragement, hadn't she? David Grantham had thought her work was worth encouraging. He'd written a glowing letter on her behalf. So had both Nathan and Carin. Her work, of course, had spoken for itself.

But it hadn't said enough. And it had been too late.

The three schools in England had told her very quickly that their enrollment was already full for the autumn session. She doubted they had even looked at her portfolio. Two had simply sent form letters. The third had suggested she apply again earlier next year.

But Italy hadn't replied. So she'd pinned all her hopes on Italy.

That was the school she had always wanted to go to anyway. It had an apprentice program where you learned by working with a master the way sculptors had often learned in the past. There, she knew, the letters of recommendation would mean little. They looked at the work you sent and decided if your talent was worth nurturing.

She'd dared to hope because it had been a dream for so long. And because she needed—desperately—to get out of Pelican Cay.

The island wasn't big enough for both her and Lachlan. Half a world seemed possibly far enough away.

And then, this afternoon, the letter had come in one thin envelope. Fiona had opened it with trembling hands.

"We find your work quite promising," the director of admissions had written, "but unfortunately limited and commercial."

Which was only the truth. Her portfolio had contained shots of her best tourist-oriented shell and driftwood sculptures, some of her metal cutout sculptures, a few sand castles and half a dozen photos showing the concept, development and plans for *The King of the Beach*. She'd got David to take photos of some smaller wood carvings and even the lumpy clay pelicans she'd done last year, and she'd sent photos of them, too.

But the dean was right. All her work was quick and commercial. She sculpted for the tourism market. It was a craft. She loved it, but she didn't labor over it. She had nothing she'd taken time with, nothing she had expended vast amounts of energy on. Nothing spectacular. Nothing noteworthy. Nothing she'd put her heart into.

Nothing except the piece she'd done of Lachlan nude.

That was the best thing she'd ever done.

But she hadn't been able to send photos of that. She had no photos. She'd promised him that no one would see it. They'd made a deal. She'd given her word.

Fiona always kept her word.

So she wasn't going to art school. But she did need to leave Pelican Cay. One look at Lachlan standing on her porch this evening had told her that.

She couldn't stay here, seeing him day after day, wanting

him the way she still wanted him, when she would always feel manipulated, when she could never trust the honesty of the feelings he had for her. She huddled in the rocking chair and tried to think.

"What am I going to do, Sparks?" she asked when he ambled over and bumped his head against her calf.

He looked at the refrigerator and then at his food bowl as if the answer were obvious.

Fiona gave a laugh that might have been a sob and got up to do his bidding. "Well, yes," she said, "but *after* dinner? Then what?"

"I CAN'T BELIEVE they didn't accept her." Molly was raging around the shop, looking like she was going to kick something.

Lachlan, who had stopped by to ask Hugh to fly him to Nassau in the morning, knew his sister well enough to stay out of her way. Besides, he wasn't displeased that they hadn't accepted Fiona. As far as he was concerned it was a reprieve of sorts.

She wasn't leaving! He had a chance with her.

"Just because she doesn't have enough traditional stuff in her portfolio," Molly groused on, banging a wrench against her palm.

"What does that mean?" Lachlan hadn't heard the reasons. He'd been too busy rejoicing to care.

"Her work is 'too consumer oriented,' they said," Molly spat, still stomping around. "It shows 'creative energy but it doesn't show commitment and discipline'! Shows what they know! If there is anyone more committed and disciplined in the world than Fiona Dunbar, I'd like to know who it is!"

Lachlan frowned. "They said that?"

"I read the letter. Idiots! So maybe she hasn't had the time to be bloody committed to her sculpture. Did they ever think of that? Maybe she's been so damned committed to people and responsibility—taking care of her dad for all those years—that she's been too busy to focus on a piece of marble or a hunk of clay. I'd like to tell them a thing or two," Molly muttered furiously. "The least they could do is give her a chance." She smacked the wrench down on the workbench, then turned on Lachlan, blessedly unarmed. "What are you doing here?"

He shook his head. "I…don't remember."

"Did you want something?"

"I… Never mind," he said vaguely and wandered back out into the dusk.

THE PHONE CALL CAME a week later.

Fiona had just dragged herself out of bed in time to go to work at the bakery. She was bleary-eyed and fuzzy-minded from tossing and turning all night, and she didn't understand the oddly accented English of the person asking to speak to her.

"Oh, ha ha. Very funny, Hugh McGillivray," she said, wishing his sense of humor were a little less juvenile and that he understood she wasn't ready to joke about it yet.

"No, zorry. You mizunderstand," the voice insisted. "I call for Mz. Dunbar. Thiz iz Luigi Bellini, Direttore di Ammissioni di Tremulini, Scuola di Dipingere e la Scultura. I call to zpeak about your enrollment."

Fiona stopped breathing.

This wasn't Hugh. She'd heard Hugh try to speak Italian once or twice. There was no way.

"Mr.—er, Signore Bellini. H-how are you?"

"I am fine. I am thinking you will be fine too because I call to tell you we have one place left. For you."

"For me?" Abruptly Fiona sat down. "In your school? When?"

"Now. I know is late but za Dutch student canzelled. We have an opening, and zo we offer ze place to you. We zee potential in you."

"You…you do?"

Sparks jumped into her lap and she clutched him desperately, hanging on to the reality of his thick short soft fur, and wondering if she was dreaming.

Signore Bellini went right on giving her the particulars about when classes started, who her master sculptor tutor would be, what she would be expected to bring and where she would live.

"I will zend you all ze information on ze e-mail to re-confirm. Classes start in two weeks. You will be here, yes?"

Fiona looked around the only home she'd ever known, then out the window across the quay to the dock, to the harbor, to everything that was familiar to her, and felt the quickening of panic in her chest.

And then she saw two of the boys, Lorenzo and Marcus, kicking a soccer ball between them as they walked down the quay. Suddenly a man swooped past, kicked the ball lightly, stealing it away from them as easily as he'd stolen her heart.

Lachlan.

Grinning at the boys, he lifted the ball on his toe, kicked it up, then bounced it on his knee to his chest and headed it into the water. The boys jumped on him and they all rolled about laughing together.

Fiona's throat tightened. Her eyes filled.

"I'm coming," she told Signore Bellini. "I'll be there."

HUGH WAS FLYING Fiona to Nassau where she would catch a plane to Frankfurt and then to Milan. From there she was getting a bus. She would have to transfer twice. But she had the Italian phrase book her brother Mike had bought for her and she was sure she'd be fine.

"Of course she'll be fine," Lachlan said gruffly when Molly reported all this again this morning. He was sitting at his desk, staring out at the beach, at the spot where *The King* had stood only a few weeks ago. He didn't miss it.

And he wouldn't miss her.

He'd made up his mind about that.

He could have taught her some Italian if she'd asked. He'd spent three years in a town not far from the one she was going to. He could have told her a lot about the area if she'd expressed any interest. She hadn't.

He hadn't heard anything directly from her at all.

He'd heard enough from Molly.

For the past seven days, ever since she'd got the news from Fiona, he had been listening to Molly crowing about her friend's talent, her accomplishments, and Molly's own supreme satisfaction that Fiona was finally getting her chance.

"Like we all had ours," Molly said with enormous satisfaction. She'd come to his office on her way to see Fiona off.

"Yeah," Lachlan said for the hundredth time and went back to reading the spec sheet for the addition on the Sandpiper that Sylvester had just faxed him.

Molly frowned, then paced his office, then stopped in front of his desk. "She's leaving in half an hour, Lachlan. Why won't you come to the dock and see her off?"

Lachlan kept right on reading. "There's no point." And he had no desire to stand there and watch her fly away.

"You could always come and stop her?"

He looked up then. "No!"

Molly sighed. "Fine. Be that way. I'll tell her you had an emergency call, that you couldn't get away, but that you're happy for her. All right? She'll want to know you're happy for her."

Lachlan doubted that. But he shrugged. "Whatever." He kept his voice neutral and his eyes on the page. They didn't stray as long as Molly stood there, nor even as her footsteps receded and he heard the inn's front door open and shut.

Only when she was gone did he lift his gaze then and stare bleakly out across the pristine sand toward the empty horizon.

He *was* happy for Fiona. Of course he was. He kept telling himself that.

He just hoped someday he believed it.

CHAPTER TEN

FIONA LOVED ITALY.

She'd always thought she would.

She was delighted with the village of Tremulini, high on a Tuscan hillside. For a Bahamian girl who didn't know hills from mountains, Italy was a revelation. Fiona was fascinated by all the ups and downs. She was thrilled with the food and spent hours prowling the markets and sampling local dishes in little trattorias.

She liked her classes, the hands-on introduction to media course—painting, drawing, sculpting and printmaking— that was required of all new students, the beginning sketching-for-sculptors class where she learned to undo all the bad habits her caricaturing had taught her, and the history-of-art-in-Italy overview, which sent her to churches and museums and town squares all over the region to absorb and reflect and study.

But she knew that when Adela Dirienzo, the sculptor with whom she would do her apprenticeship, returned from teaching master classes in Amsterdam, her work would really begin.

That was fine with her. Fiona was determined to be a sponge, soaking everything up, cramming each day full to the brim with new sights, new sounds, new ideas, new friends.

Since she'd arrived a month ago, she had made a lot of new friends at school—Roberto from her sketching class, and Hans and Resi from her history class, and Maria,

Guillermo and Dmitri from her media course. She'd made friends in the community as well. Giulia, the registrar's secretary, had taken her under her wing, had found her a tiny flat above the wine shop her uncle Tommaso ran. Her uncle Pietro, a waiter in the local trattoria, plied Fiona with forty flavors of gelato and introduced her to other local delicacies, and Giulia's cousins, Vittorio, Alberto, Franco, Giancarlo, Sophia and Marcelo took her into their lives and made her a part of the family.

And a good thing, too, because Fiona needed family. Desperately.

For as much as she loved Italy and her friends and her classes and all she was experiencing and learning, and as much as she looked forward to learning from Signora Dirienzo, she was homesick, too.

She kept her days as full as she possibly could.

But her nights were long and filled with memories.

Nights brought dreams of soft pink sand beaches and warm turquoise seas, of conch fritters and pineapple soda and ice-cold beer, of pastel-colored houses and white picket fences and potholed streets.

And not just food and places, but faces.

People.

Mike and Claire and Tom and Peter. Paul and Julie and their new twins, Alison and Jack who had been barely three weeks old when Fiona had left. Maurice and Estelle and their family. Carin, Nathan, Lacey and Josh. Miss Saffron. Tony. Nikki. Molly. Hugh.

Lachlan.

She couldn't sleep for remembering Lachlan. Wanting Lachlan.

Loving Lachlan.

It was stupid and she knew it. But there it was: she'd come halfway around the world and hadn't left him behind at all.

It was early days yet, she told herself. She'd barely been

gone a month. Surely by Christmas she wouldn't be dreaming of him every night. She wouldn't be thinking of him a thousand times a day.

If she was, she couldn't possibly go home for the holiday. She would have to go with Resi and Hans to Innsbruck to go skiing. A little island girl like her going skiing in Austria? The mind boggled. But then hadn't there been a Jamaican bobsled team?

She was out in the world doing things, learning things, growing and getting a life. And someday, God willing, Lachlan would be only a small insignificant memory.

She was sure she already was that to him.

She didn't believe that once she had left, he had wasted a moment's thought on her. He'd wanted her. He'd had her.

End of story.

To make sure it really *was* the end of the story, she made it a point to go out on the occasional date with Vittorio, one of Giulia's cousins.

Vittorio was lively, intense and the stereotypical "Italian lover." He was perennially ready to sweep her off her feet. Fiona found him fun and charming and had no intention of getting serious about him. But if she went out with him, at least she could write home about it.

She spent a lot of time writing home. She sent e-mails several times a week, telling her brothers and sisters-in-law and Carin and Molly all about the places she went and the people she met.

She wrote about her classes and her teachers, about her classmates and her friends, about going shopping in the markets and getting her hair cut by the old lady who lived around the corner, and the sculptures she saw in the museums she went to, and what fun riding a motorbike was.

And because she wanted them to know she wasn't pining, because she wanted them to believe that she really was happy and glad that she'd gone—even though some nights she ached with longing for home and for Lachlan—she made her life sound even fuller—especially of Vittorio—than it was.

LACHLAN TRIED TO BE HAPPY for her. And most of the time he honest-to-God was. He knew she needed to have a chance to spread her wings, to see the big wide world.

He could wait, he told himself. It wouldn't be that long until she came back to Pelican Cay. Two years wasn't forever. She was doing what she wanted to do. Having the life she wanted to have. At last.

And him?

He got by. He threw himself into renovations. He spent a lot of time at the Sandpiper because it was easier than being lonely on Pelican Cay. He bought another inn in the Caicos and began work down there. When he was home he helped Hugh finish the shop and put a new roof on the Mirabelle, his other local inn.

When he wasn't working, he spent his time with the kids on the soccer team. They were still practicing three times a week and playing in tournaments on other islands. He loved working with them. They kept him sharp, they kept him honest. Most of the time they kept him smiling.

He was okay as long as he had occasional fixes—news of what Fiona was doing.

Of course she wasn't writing to him. But he got his fixes anyway. He stopped by now and then to admire Julie and Paul's twins, and Julie always eagerly volunteered information on how Fiona was doing.

"She's learning so much," Julie told him. "And she sent me a scan of a sketch she did of her media professor. Want to see?"

"Sure." He tried not to look as avid as he felt.

The sketch had obviously been dashed off in a few minutes. But it captured the man—his beaky nose and slouchy beret, his sweater with the holes in the elbows, his slightly stooped posture, but the intent look in his eyes said he knew what he was talking about. Fiona got at the heart of people.

"It's very good." It was wonderful.

"Want it?" Julie asked. "I can print another for us."

"Well." God, he wanted it so badly his hand was shaking. "I guess." He went away, carrying it, aching with loneliness, missing her more than he thought possible.

She wrote to Claire and Mike and the boys, too. He had less reason to stop by their place. But Tom sometimes told him what she was doing.

"She went to a soccer game with Vittorio," he reported eagerly. "She said she saw where you used to play."

"Did she?" He felt a twisting in his midsection as he wished he could have shown the city to her. When he thought back on the time he was there, he came up with a lot of places he would have liked to have taken her there. He wondered if this Vittorio guy knew the places he did. He hoped not.

Carin told him Fiona was learning a lot about art history. "Going to museums every weekend," she said.

He hadn't spent a lot of time in museums when he'd lived there. "I wouldn't mind doing that," he said to Carin. "I never had anyone to go with either."

"Oh, she's not alone," Carin said blithely. "She always goes with Vittorio."

"Does she?" Lachlan's jaw got tight.

He dropped by Hugh's every day when he was on the island. He saw Molly every afternoon.

Molly told him when Fiona had moved into her flat above the wine shop. "Her friend Giulia found it for her," Molly said. "And they all helped her move in—Alberto, Franco, Giancarlo, Vittorio."

Vittorio again.

Molly told him about Fiona's interest in church architecture. "She's learning a lot. Checking out the churches in all the villages."

"Taking buses?" Lachlan grinned, remembering the old buses.

But Molly shook her head. "She bought a motorbike. Since she got it, they go all over, she and Vittorio."

And now Molly said Fiona was going to Milan for the weekend.

"Milan? On the motorbike? By herself?" Lachlan was appalled. Fiona was a small town girl. Thinking of her coping with a city the size of Milan was unnerving.

"Oh, no," Molly said. "Vittorio drives a Ferrari."

Lachlan had only one question: Who the hell was Vittorio?

THE FIRST WEEK in October Fiona's master teacher, Adela Dirienzo, returned from Amsterdam.

It was just as well, Fiona thought, that Signora Dirienzo hadn't been there when she first arrived. The learning curve was high enough with only her regular classes. If she had been plunged straight into one-on-one work with a master she might have panicked.

Even now, with four weeks' work under her belt Fiona was nervous. Since she'd arrived she'd seen plenty of examples of Signora Dirienzo's work. It was strong, powerful, dynamic. She worked in both marble and clay, creating works that were substantial and yet that pulsated with life.

She was, the direttore, Luigi Bellini, told Fiona when she arrived, the reason they had admitted her.

"She say you have talent," Signore Bellini told her. "She zees potential in the pictures you zent. She wants to nurture your talent. Develop it."

Potential? In the pelicans? In the sand castles? Maybe in the cutout surfers and fishermen. They were dynamic at least.

"Signora Dirienzo knows what she's talking about," Hans, her friend from the history class, told her.

Fiona dearly hoped so. And at the same time she was apprehensive about her first meeting. What if it had been a mistake? What if Signora Dirienzo had mistaken someone else's portfolio for Fiona's? What if they'd sent her the wrong pictures when she was in Amsterdam?

So it was with considerable trepidation that she mounted the stairs to the signora's studio on Wednesday afternoon and knocked on the door.

"Come in!" The words were Italian, but Fiona understood them now.

She pushed open the door to find a sixtyish woman dressed like a workman, her long salt-and-pepper hair dragged back into a knot at the base of her neck, as she wrestled with a block of marble. She looked up at Fiona's entrance and beamed.

"Ah, you are the island girl? Fiona, yes? Come help me, *per favore*. This is ours." She patted the marble as if it were an old friend.

Fiona dropped her backpack on the floor and hurried to do as she was told. There wasn't time to worry. There was only time to respond.

Signora Dirienzo—"Adela! You call me Adela," her teacher said as she and Fiona moved the chunk of marble into place—believed in jumping right in. "Is what I like about you. Energy," she said. "Always energy. You see potential, yes?"

"Um, I try," Fiona said.

"You look here. You see?" Signora Dirienzo—Adela— moved her hands over the marble, stroked it, seemed to shape it as her palms caressed the grain. Fiona tried to see. She nodded her head, feeling as if she was completely out of her depth.

"You touch," Adela said. "You feel. Then you see? Yes?"

Fiona touched. The stone was cool against her fingers. Not as smooth as she would have thought. There was a grain. A texture.

"Yes, yes. Like that." Adela nodded, smiling. "Come." She plucked at Fiona's sleeve. "Here. You feel." And she practically dragged Fiona over to the finished pieces that sat on shelves and in deep window ledges. "Close your eyes."

Fiona closed them.

"Now," Adela said, taking her hands and putting them on a piece of sculpture. "Feel."

Fiona felt. She ran her hands over it, felt the smoothness one way, the grain the other, ran her fingers lightly over angles and bends and curves. She did it on a dozen pieces, possibly more.

"Which one you are feeling?" Adela demanded. "What is it?"

And, eyes closed, Fiona tried to describe what she was feeling.

"Yes, yes! Exactly. Yes! You see! But you do not need eyes to see!" Adela beamed, then tugged her onward. "Come. You feel this next."

They moved around the room from piece to piece. Under Adela's direction, she felt them all, marble and terra-cotta, large and small, clothed and naked. And Fiona was reminded of her sculpture of Lachlan. A flush heated her cheeks.

"Ah, yes. You feel passion." Adela laughed delightedly when she spotted Fiona's blush. "That is what we want, what we nurture! That I cannot teach. That you must bring, yes?" She smiled, her intent blue gaze settling on Fiona. Then she let out a long, satisfied sigh. "That I know you bring."

"You do?"

Adela nodded. "Oh, yes. Come now. We get to work."

The rest of the two-hour session was as intense as the beginning. The chunk of marble was theirs, she told Fiona. They would learn it together. They would feel it and talk about it and try to understand what it said.

"The stones speak," Adela told her. "But they need us to give them voice. We must listen and feel and then show what they say."

Avidly Fiona listened while Adela lectured on. Listening to Adela was like being given a translator. Ever since she'd been sculpting, Fiona had been trying to find the words in this new idiom. Now, at last, with Adela she had someone to teach her what the words meant and how to say them. She had the mentor she'd told Lachlan she needed.

"I only help," Adela insisted when they were finishing.

Fiona's mind was spinning, full of new ideas, new concepts, new ways of looking at her medium and the world. She didn't know whether she was more exhilarated or exhausted. "I just hope I'm up to it," she said.

"You already have the tools. I refine them. You have the passion, as I say."

"How do you know?" Fiona asked. She thought she did, but she wasn't sure.

"I see it in your work, this passion."

"In the shells? In the cutouts? In *The King of the Beach?*"

Adela smiled. "Is that what you call him?"

Fiona nodded.

"He is the king, yes," Adela agreed, nodding as she opened a wide flat drawer in the map cabinet behind her, then took out Fiona's flat black portfolio and spread out some photos.

"Passion, yes?" she said happily.

Fiona stared. They weren't photos of *The King of the Beach*. They were photos of her sculpture of Lachlan!

Closeups showing every side, every curve, every line of the sculpture of Lachlan as beautiful and naked as Fiona remembered him.

She went white. "Who? How——? How did you——?"

"King of the beach indeed." Adela's gaze flicked up and her eyes laughed. Then she mused, "He looks familiar. But then all beautiful men, we wish they look familiar, yes?"

It was all Fiona could do not to snatch the photos and bury them. How on earth——?

Her mind was reeling.

Had Molly? But Molly didn't know. No one knew—
Except the man himself.

IT COULDN'T HAVE BEEN LACHLAN.

He would never!

So it had to have been Molly, Fiona had decided by the
time she got home that afternoon.

Molly must have found the sculpture wherever Lachlan
had put it. Surely it hadn't been out for display. But if she'd
stumbled across it, Molly—knowing how upset Fiona
was—would have known how much she'd been depending
on being able to leave Pelican Cay. She must have taken
matters into her own hands, making the photos and sending
them in.

Dear God.

What on earth would Lachlan do when he found out?

The sound of the door buzzer from downstairs momentarily interrupted her panic attack. She'd been pacing the
floor since she'd got home.

"Come out for a coffee?" Vittorio had urged her. "Tell
me about your meeting with Signora Dirienzo."

But Fiona had shaken her head. "I can't," she'd bab-
bled. "I need—I need to think!"

Maybe Lachlan would never find out. Maybe it would
never come up. But Signora Dirienzo had talked about
doing a show at some point. "Where you've been and
where you're going." And she'd patted Lachlan's clay self
on the butt. "Starting here." She'd beamed.

The buzzer went again. Longer. More insistently.

Fiona knew who it was. Marcelo, another of Giulia's
cousins, the eldest of Tommaso's sons, had said he'd stop
by after work to replace a cracked windowpane.

If she wasn't involved in something, Marcelo would talk
her ear off. And she didn't need to talk to Marcelo right
now.

She needed to think what she was going to do, how she

was going to handle this. Molly, of course, wouldn't have known about Fiona's promise to Lachlan.

The buzzer again.

"Come up!" Fiona yelled. Then she deliberately ducked her head under the tap to wash her hair so she could ignore Marcelo when the door opened.

"It's over there," she said, waving her hand toward the broken window sash without looking up when she heard footsteps at the top of the stairs. "Can you fix it?"

"Maybe," a voice said. "I'll try."

Fiona whipped her head around, flinging water everywhere.

Lachlan was standing in the door.

"You've cut your hair." He was staring at her, looking a bit dazed himself.

Fiona stared right back, stunned. She must be dreaming. Water dripped into her eyes. She shook her head.

Lachlan? Here?

Then all of a sudden she realized *why* he must be here, and her stomach dropped. Oh God.

"Did Molly tell you what she did?" she said frantically, grabbing for a towel, scrubbing at her wet hair. "I didn't ask her to, I swear it! I—"

"Molly? What did Molly do?" Lachlan looked perplexed.

"Took the photos! The photos of the sculpture! Of you! I just found out about them today. Honest to God, Lachlan, I didn't break my word. I didn't take them. I didn't send them in!"

"I did."

Her jaw dropped. She stared at him. "*You* sent them?" Her knees threatened to buckle. She clutched the back of one of the kitchen chairs for support. "But…but *why?*"

He shrugged. "You wanted to go to school. You never got to."

Her mind reeled. "Yes, but—"

"I owed you," Lachlan said quietly. He swallowed, shut

his eyes for just a moment, then opened them and met her astonished gaze. "For the net," he told her. "For doing it for the wrong reasons."

"It's not—"

"I love you."

Fiona couldn't say anything to that. She could only stare.

Every instinct she had told her not to believe it, that this was Lachlan who couldn't be trusted.

But a Lachlan who couldn't be trusted would never have taken those photos. He would certainly never have sent them to the school. That Lachlan would never have offered himself up for her benefit. That Lachlan had been out for himself—not her.

And this Lachlan?

She opened her mouth, but no sound came out.

"I love you," he said again. His voice was still quiet, but she heard pain in it. "I don't know if you believe it or not," he told her. "I hope you do. I hope you will. I'll do what I can to prove it to you."

"I—" she managed that much.

But he went on hurriedly, "I don't expect you to come back to Pelican Cay. I speak a little Italian. I thought I might hang around a little. Maybe teach some soccer here. Get a job at a school? While you're in school…if you're interested…I know it's the first chance you've had to spread your wings, to try something new, to…"

"I love you, too."

She needed to say that now, right off the bat, because if she didn't she might not be able to before she started crying. Her throat ached and tightened. Her eyes swam.

She believed. She trusted.

"Fiona—" He started to interrupt her, but this time she wouldn't let him. She closed the space between them and put her fingers against his lips.

"I don't want any of those things," she told him, "as much as I want you."

He buried his face in her sopping hair and wrapped his

arms around her. A shudder ran through him. And Fiona, who knew all about feeling after two hours with Signora Dirienzo today, reveled in the feel of the hard strong body pressed against hers. She relished the whiskery roughness of his unshaven cheek on her own. She delighted in the press of his lips, the touch of his tongue.

Her own lips parted to welcome him. Her arms went around him, locking against the taut muscles of his back.

She felt it all. She felt absolutely wonderful!

The nice thing about living in a one-room flat was that it was only steps to the bed. They got there in half a dozen steps, tugging zips, fumbling with buttons, shedding clothes all the way, falling on to the mattress, tangled together.

And then there was nothing between them but the rush to completion, they stopped and pulled back, not touching. Just looking.

Their gazes met.

Then their hands touched.

Then slowly they began to move. Stroking, learning. *Feeling.*

Oh God, yes.

Signora Dirienzo—Adela—was right.

Fiona had passion. Passion for this man who had done the unthinkable for her. "I'm sorry I doubted you," she whispered. "I didn't know! I didn't trust."

"I didn't give you much reason to." Lachlan's words were a breath against her lips. "I didn't mean to hurt you. I wanted to help you. Really. It was manipulative, I admit it. But I wanted you to realize what I already knew—that we belonged together."

"I did know it," she told him, smiling. "I've known that since I was nine years old."

"You never!"

"Did so!"

"Did not!"

"Did so!"

So much for gentle touching and tender reverence. They

rolled together, laughing, clutching, slipping, sliding, locking together. Moving.

Loving.

Loving each other. And together they shattered—and became whole at the very same time.

"I WASN'T KIDDING," Lachlan said later after Fiona had taken him to the trattoria for pasta with oil and garlic, salad and three kinds of gelato for dessert. It was good, but better was being with her. He smiled at all the introductions she made—to Pietro and to Giulia and assorted Italian cousins, one of whom turned out to be the mysterious Vittorio. Lachlan could afford to be polite to him now. "I'm here to stay."

"But the Moonstone!" Fiona protested. "And the Sandpiper! And—"

"I can deal with them. Honest." Lachlan put a hand over his heart. "I learned my lesson," he told her solemnly. "I meant what I said earlier. I can do what I need to do from here for as long as you want to stay."

Fiona stared at him. "Are you...sure?"

He nodded. "This is your chance. Your talent. Your dream. I got to go after mine. Now it's your turn. I'll fly back as often as I need to. We'll fly home to get married, but then we'll come back. Okay?"

"Married?" she echoed, looking stricken.

"What did you think? That you were going to get to be my mistress forever?" He laughed nervously. "Or that I wasn't going to insist you make an honest man of me? I don't want the world thinking I let any old woman sculpt me naked."

Fiona laughed. "My teacher thought you looked familiar."

"Yeah, well, that's all the view she gets. I'm saving myself for my wife. So," he prompted because she still hadn't responded, "what's your answer?"

He knew an eternity's panic in a moment. What if she didn't—?

"Answer? Oh, Lachlan!" she cried and launched herself into his arms.

He caught her, held her, nuzzled her neck. His heart began beating again. He began breathing again. He kissed her soundly and gave a laugh that felt perilously close to a sob. "I take it that's a yes?"

"Yes," she said, putting him out of his misery. She kissed him hard. "Oh, yes!"

THE WEDDING TOOK PLACE at Christmas in the tiny turquoise church on Pelican Cay's highest hill. Not much of a hill if you had just come from Tuscany. But it was home, and it was beautiful, and for the ceremony the whole island crowded in.

Hugh didn't wear a tie, but he did put on shoes to be best man. Molly, as Fiona's maid of honor, scrubbed the grease off her hands, borrowed a dress from Carin and actually looked like a girl. The entire soccer team served as ushers and bridesmaids. David Grantham brought a tour along to witness a bit of island culture. Adela came, she told Fiona, to see what the groom looked like with clothes on. Some of Lachlan's soccer teammates were there, too.

"Seeing is believing," Lars Eric Lindquist said cheerfully.

It was a lovely wedding. Fiona had planned it all and Lachlan had let her. He'd only drawn the line when she'd suggested doing an ice sculpture of him. Nude.

Sparks didn't go to the wedding. But since he'd been staying at the Moonstone with Suzette while Fiona was in Italy, he did attend the reception. He passed up the wedding cake, but dined on lobster, crab cakes and conch chowder before retiring to a spot in the sun.

"That cat's got it made," Lachlan told Fiona, watching Sparks amble outside and claim a quiet secluded spot out of the way of all the noisy revelers who were eating and drinking and dancing and playing soccer and volleyball on the beach.

Lachlan was all for a party—and this one would certainly go down in the annals of Pelican Cay's most glorious parties for years and years to come—but there ought to be a time limit. Especially when a man had been waiting all day to be alone with his wife.

"You're not enjoying yourself?" Fiona asked. She was nibbling on a piece of wedding cake. Her face was flushed and her eyes were alight and she looked, to Lachlan, like the most beautiful desirable woman in the world.

"Yeah, but I'd be enjoying myself more if it was just the two of us," he said honestly.

Fiona set the cake down and took his hand. "Let's go, then."

"Go?" He blinked, astonished, then looked around at the party still in full swing around them. "Now?"

Fiona looked around, too, then shrugged. "They won't miss us. They're well occupied, I'm sure. And I have a surprise for you." She grinned.

"What surprise?"

"You'll see!" She grabbed his hand and pulled him toward the door.

Bemused, Lachlan allowed himself to be pulled. Surprise? Undoubtedly. Fiona never failed to surprise him.

"You rented us a room at the Mirabelle?" he guessed.

She shook her head and led him down the path through the mangroves. "We're going to my place." She was dancing along in her long white wedding dress, like a wedding cake on the move.

Grinning, Lachlan followed her. "You've stocked up enough food for a week so we don't have to get out of bed?" he said hopefully.

"No surprise there." Fiona grinned over her shoulder. They got through the mangroves and when they came to the top of Bonefish Road she turned and ran to the sculpture by the cricket grounds. There she unpinned her veil and tossed it up. *The King* caught it on his outstretched hand.

"You didn't find that on the beach," Lachlan told her.

Fiona laughed. "Artistic license! Come on."

She began to run again, dress streaming out behind her. And Lachlan ran after her through deserted streets. The whole island was still at the Moonstone celebrating their wedding.

"I've got it," he said when he caught up with her on the porch of her house.

"Got what?" Fiona pushed open the door and started to go in, but Lachlan grabbed her and scooped her into his arms.

"What the surprise is," he told her as he carried her over the threshold and right up the stairs to her bedroom.

"Oh yes?" Fiona smiled as he laid her gently on the bed and wondered how he was ever going to have the patience to undo all those hundred buttons.

"Yes," he said because he could take her teasing now. "You're wearing a pair of red panties under this getup."

Fiona grinned and opened her arms to him. "Actually," she said, "I'm not. That's your surprise. I'm not wearing anything at all!"

✂ **Your opinion is important to us!** Please take a few moments to share your thoughts with us about your experiences with Harlequin and Silhouette books. Your comments will be very useful in ensuring that we deliver books you love to read.
Please take a few minutes to complete the questionnaire,
then send it to us at the address below.

Send your completed questionnaires to:
Harlequin/Silhouette Reader Survey, P.O. Box 9046, Buffalo, NY 14269-9046

---

1. As you may know, there are many different lines under the Harlequin and Silhouette brands. Each of the lines is listed below. Please check the box that most represents your reading habit for each line.

Line	Currently read this line	Do not read this line	Not sure if I read this line
Harlequin American Romance	❏	❏	❏
Harlequin Duets	❏	❏	❏
Harlequin Romance	❏	❏	❏
Harlequin Historicals	❏	❏	❏
Harlequin Superromance	❏	❏	❏
Harlequin Intrigue	❏	❏	❏
Harlequin Presents	❏	❏	❏
Harlequin Temptation	❏	❏	❏
Harlequin Blaze	❏	❏	❏
Silhouette Special Edition	❏	❏	❏
Silhouette Romance	❏	❏	❏
Silhouette Intimate Moments	❏	❏	❏
Silhouette Desire	❏	❏	❏

2. Which of the following best describes why you bought *this book?* One answer only, please.

the picture on the cover	❏	the title	❏
the author	❏	the line is one I read often	❏
part of a miniseries	❏	saw an ad in another book	❏
saw an ad in a magazine/newsletter	❏	a friend told me about it	❏
I borrowed/was given this book	❏	other: _____	❏

3. Where did you buy *this book?* One answer only, please.

at Barnes & Noble	❏	at a grocery store	❏
at Waldenbooks	❏	at a drugstore	❏
at Borders	❏	on eHarlequin.com Web site	❏
at another bookstore	❏	from another Web site	❏
at Wal-Mart	❏	Harlequin/Silhouette Reader	❏
at Target	❏	Service/through the mail	
at Kmart	❏	used books from anywhere	❏
at another department store or mass merchandiser	❏	I borrowed/was given this book	❏

4. On average, how many Harlequin and Silhouette books do you buy at one time?

I buy _____ books at one time ❏
I rarely buy a book ❏

MRQ403HP-1A

5. How many times per month do you shop for any *Harlequin and/or Silhouette* books?
One answer only, please.

1 or more times a week	❏	a few times per year	❏
1 to 3 times per month	❏	less often than once a year	❏
1 to 2 times every 3 months	❏	never	❏

6. When you think of your ideal heroine, which *one* statement describes her the best?
One answer only, please.

She's a woman who is strong-willed	❏	She's a desirable woman	❏
She's a woman who is needed by others	❏	She's a powerful woman	❏
She's a woman who is taken care of	❏	She's a passionate woman	❏
She's an adventurous woman	❏	She's a sensitive woman	❏

7. The following statements describe types or genres of books that you may be
interested in reading. Pick *up to 2 types* of books that you are most interested in.

I like to read about truly romantic relationships	❏
I like to read stories that are sexy romances	❏
I like to read romantic comedies	❏
I like to read a romantic mystery/suspense	❏
I like to read about romantic adventures	❏
I like to read romance stories that involve family	❏
I like to read about a romance in times or places that I have never seen	❏
Other: _____	❏

*The following questions help us to group your answers with those readers who are
similar to you. Your answers will remain confidential.*

8. Please record your year of birth below.

19 ____

9. What is your marital status?

single ❏   married ❏   common-law ❏   widowed ❏
divorced/separated ❏

10. Do you have children 18 years of age or younger currently living at home?

yes ❏   no ❏

11. Which of the following best describes your employment status?

employed full-time or part-time ❏   homemaker ❏   student ❏
retired ❏   unemployed ❏

12. Do you have access to the Internet from either home or work?

yes ❏   no ❏

13. Have you ever visited eHarlequin.com?

yes ❏   no ❏

14. What state do you live in?

_____

15. Are you a member of Harlequin/Silhouette Reader Service?

yes ❏   Account # _____   no ❏   MRQ403HP-1B

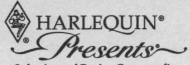

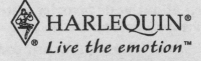

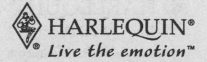

The world's bestselling romance series.

HARLEQUIN®
Presents

Seduction and Passion Guaranteed!

INTERNATIONAL
DOCTORS

They're guaranteed to raise your pulse!

Meet the most eligible medical men of the world, in a new series of stories, by popular authors, that will make your heart race!

Whether they're saving lives or dealing with desire, our doctors have got bedside manners that send temperatures soaring....

Coming in Harlequin Presents in 2003:

THE DOCTOR'S SECRET CHILD by Catherine Spencer
#2311, on sale March

THE PASSION TREATMENT by Kim Lawrence
#2330, on sale June

THE DOCTOR'S RUNAWAY BRIDE by Sarah Morgan
#2366, on sale December

Pick up a Harlequin Presents® novel and you will enter a world of spine-tingling passion and provocative, tantalizing romance!

Available wherever Harlequin books are sold.

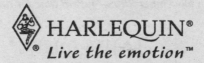

HARLEQUIN®
Live the emotion™

Visit us at www.eHarlequin.com